Sarita, Be Brave

by

Ruby C. Tolliver

EAKIN PRESS 🎭 Austin, Texas

FIRST EDITION

Published in the United States of America
By Eakin Press
A Division of Sunbelt Media, Inc.
P.O. Box 90159
Austin, TX 78709
email: eakinpub@sig.net
www.eakinpress.com

2 3 4 5 6 7 8 9

1-57168-184-1

Library of Congress Cataloging-in-Publication Data

Tolliver, Ruby C.
    Sarita, be brave / by Ruby C. Tolliver.
        p.   cm.
    Summary: When political unrest in Honduras forces twelve-year-old Sara to flee
with her family and make the dangerous journey north to Texas, she faces the chal-
lenges of starting a new school and a new life.
    ISBN 1-57168-184-1 (hard)
    1. Honduran Americans—Juvenile fiction.   [1. Honduran Americans—Fiction.
2. Emigration and immigration—Fiction.   3. Schools—Fiction.   4. Texas—
Fiction.]   I. Title
PZ7.T5748Sar   1999
    [Fic]--dc21   3/00   98-48356
    [B]   CIP
                                                                            AC

To Doug and Johanna Baldwin
and the other volunteers who teach English
as a Second Language to those who need it.

Chapter One

"Hurry! Ronaldo is coming!" Sara's father, Adan, called from the driveway. "Bring your rifle and ammunition. I will find a place in the truck for them." Twelve-year-old Sara, with her rifle and box of ammunition, stepped outside the white painted adobe house.

She stared through the September morning twilight toward the oncoming truck. "We really are going," she whispered. Until this moment she had thought her father might change his mind. He loved Honduras. After Sara's birth in Texas, he had brought his family back to live in his native country. But now, since the rebels were infiltrating even the mountains, Adan was ready to return to Texas where she and the twins would be safe.

"Sara?" Adan called again. "Over here." She walked to where he stood by their belongings and placed her rifle and the ammunition box on the ground. "Now, Sara, go wake the twins."

1

Sara went inside and shook each twin and said, "Get up. Ronaldo is coming." The six-year-old twins were up and running to the kitchen table. They had slept in their traveling clothes. Sara handed them the tortillas and cheese. There was only water to drink, but the excited twins did not complain. They stuffed the food into their mouths and ran to gather the small bundles that held their toys. *They are as excited as I am*, Sara thought as she glanced around the long, narrow room. *What a difference this move is from the one we made three years ago.* So much sadness, then. They had come up the mountain to bury her mother and the new baby who had died, too. They had stayed to live with her grandmother because her father had needed help with the three-year-old twins.

Sara remembered those days of sadness—to lose her mother—to move to the mountain—to leave Tegucigalapa where so many of their relatives lived. She remembered the many tears she had shed when leaving school friends she would never see again.

Now that her grandmother had died, this would not be a sad leaving. She knew she would miss her grandmother who had died three months earlier, but she would not miss the students of the small, one-room schoolhouse down in the village at the foot of the mountain. The girls were too young to be her friends. She was glad she would not have to walk the lonely two miles through the forest anymore.

The first thing Adan had done when they settled in the adobe house was to trade for a .22 rifle for her. Sara was afraid to use the rifle. "You want to go to school, don't you Sara?" Adan asked. "If you go, you will have to take the rifle. The road down is only a wide trail. There are snakes, jaguars, wild pigs, and other wild animals in the forest."

"But, Papa—"

"Do not worry, little one. I will teach you to use the rifle." And he had taught her. She no longer feared the rifle. She had practiced until she could hit the center of the target every time.

Grandmother at first protested. "She is only nine years old, Adan."

"No, Mamacita, she is not too young. The rifle you gave me when I was that age was heavier than the .22. Yet, I learned to use it. If she goes down the mountain to school, she takes the rifle."

When his mother still complained, he said, "There are bad men prowling our country. Suppose a thief came to our home. Would you use the rifle to protect the children?"

"No, Adan. I could not pull the trigger. You know that."

He laughed. "Yes, I know that. You are too tender-hearted to wring the neck of the old rooster. I am teaching Sara to be brave."

Down in the city, Adan had worked in a factory. On the mountain, he had become a logger. He knew the forest and the snakes and animals that lived in the forest. He also knew Sara would be the only one to provide protection for the family while he was at work deep in the forest.

The noise of the approaching truck made Sara quickly pack the tortillas, rice, and beans she had cooked the night before. She placed them in the box with the cooking pots and dishes. They would have to cook their meals on the journey. "Papa!" she called. "The food box is ready." It was too heavy for her to carry.

3

While she waited for her father to come she walked through the three rooms of the house. She stared at the familiar wall hangings and religious pictures, which had been the possessions of her grandmother. She shrugged away a tinge of regret at having to leave them. *I will not start crying. It would upset Papa to see me. When I get to Texas I will never cry again.* She wondered if anyone cried in Texas. *I must not think of that,* she decided.

She looked around the rooms to see if she had forgotten anything. The furniture would be left for the next occupant. There was no room in the camper shell of the truck for furniture. When she had asked if they could take her mother's small desk, Adan had said, "We are lucky to have a ride to Texas."

"But, take no furniture?"

"The house of my brother has furniture. We will manage."

Sara tied her scarf securely about her head. She had braided her long black hair the night before. The roads they would take down the mountain to the Pan-American Highway would be dusty.

At first she had not wanted to go to Texas. Even on the maps Texas seemed to be far away and very big. Then when her friend Cuahutemoe and his family, the Ramirezes, had gone north to avoid the war, she was ready to leave, too. The Ramirezes had been their nearest neighbor. Now, no one lived near them.

She paused to stare out the window at the three crosses in the tiny, enclosed cemetery. One stood on the grave of her grandfather. The new mound of dirt with its freshly painted cross was the grave of her grandmother. The other cross, the one with the faded plastic flowers, marked the grave of her mother holding the baby.

4

The priest from the village had blessed the mountainside site and permitted the burials. Sara knew there were also the two unmarked graves of babies of her grandmother. *Who will now tend the graves?* Sara wondered.

Sara had learned to manage the household after her grandmother became ill and then died. At that time, her father had said, "We will stay here until the season for cutting timber is over." But last week, Ronaldo, her father's nephew, came with news from the city.

"They are taking all the men to become soldiers. I do not wish to fight. Lupe and I are going back to Texas. My papa will help us. We will stay with the sister of Lupe and her family in Houston. Anyway," he smiled, "there is much work there and we want the baby to be born in Texas."

Uncle Frank Beltran was the father of Ronaldo and the brother of Adan. Frank and Adan had received their United States citizenship before each had married. They had worked the docks in Houston. Ronaldo, who had been born in Texas, would be allowed to work there. Sara, also, was born in Texas. The twins were born after Adan had brought his family back to Honduras. There had been many papers to fill out from both governments to allow them all to return and live in Texas.

Sara ran outside as Ronaldo braked his old pickup truck in a swirl of dust. She placed their bed rolls in the truck. Her father loaded the water can and the two cans of gasoline. The twins, Hosea and Ester, squealed with excitement as they ran around getting in the way of the others. Lupe waddled into the house making sure the cupboards were empty.

Adan placed the box of food behind the seat of

the truck. Rolando and Lupe's belongings were piled high at the front of the camper. Rolando was inside the camper spreading sleeping mats for the children to sit or sleep on. Blankets were folded nearby. Sara handed Rolando the straw-filled pillows.

Adan placed the three satchels that held their belongings in the truck. One contained his work clothes and an extra pair of boots. One held the children's clothes. The smallest satchel held Sara's most prized possessions—her mother's wedding dress and the family pictures.

Rolando, Adan, and Lupe would ride up front. Adan lifted and placed the twins in the camper. Sara climbed in by herself. Adan put his hands on the shoulder of each twin. "Sara will be in charge. Knock on the window if you need something." He kissed each child, then added, "Do not bother Ronaldo unless it is important. He has to watch the road across the mountains."

Finally, everything was loaded. "Now, we go," Ronaldo said as he crossed himself.

The twins began to argue over which mat they would take. Sara finally decided for them. "You may change places when we cross the mountains." Ester and Hosea were soon curled up on the mats and sound asleep. The straw-filled pillows and mats kept their heads from cracking against the metal bed of the truck. Sara wondered at their ability to sleep on such a bumpy road. She was glad they slept during the scary descent down the mountainside, especially where part of the road had slid off into the rocks below.

The sun was at its zenith when Ronaldo pulled to a stop under an overhanging cliff. Lupe got out to stretch. Sara was no longer embarrassed for her.

"The baby is pressing low," Lupe explained. "Two more weeks to go," she said and sighed, *"ay mi."*

After they had eaten their tortillas and beans, Ronaldo waved them back into the truck. The afternoon passed as they continued on their journey. That night Adan took over the driving. Ronaldo and Lupe slept in the back with the twins. Sara sat in the front with her father. The first day had ended.

Three days and nights had gone by and they were deep into Mexico. They had lost three hours at the Guatemalan border securing visas, and two more hours crossing the border into Mexico. Lupe was complaining about the heat and not being able to bathe.

"At the next river crossing we will bathe," Ronaldo promised. Sara and the twins were tired and dirty, too.

"Please get us a room in a hotel where we can bathe and sleep," Sara whispered to her father. "I do not like the thought of bathing in the river in front of people." She knew there was always a cantina at the river crossings.

"We do not have money to spend on hotels," her father said. "I do not know how long it will be before I find work." Sara did not ask again. She knew he spoke the truth.

They stopped by a river that afternoon. Sara, Ester, and Lupe walked around a bend in the river to where the trees on shore shielded them from the cantina customers. Sara refused to remove her clothes. She washed as best she could. It felt so good to take down her braids and wash her dusty hair. When Lupe, who also had kept her clothes on as she bathed, was ready to return to the truck, Sara toweled Ester and helped her dress in clean clothes.

Then, she dried her hair. She wrapped a towel around her wet dress before she hurried to the truck.

First, Lupe climbed into the truck. The men held a blanket to shield her while she put on dry clothes. Then Sara changed. While the men left to bathe, Sara hung the wet clothes on a line inside the camper shell. The men, not so modest, stripped and went into the water behind the trees. Adan rolled their dirty clothes into a ball. "Put these behind the gasoline cans. You then will not notice how bad they smell." Sara and the twins laughed, for it felt so good to be clean and in fresh clothing.

Ronaldo began to complain about the loss of time. "We will eat on the road," he said. "Lupe, roll some beans in the tortillas. When the children get hungry, they can eat as we ride. You and I and Adan will eat before we sleep."

"Papa, I feel so sorry for you," Sara whispered. "When have you slept?" A frown puckered her brow as she leaned against him.

He hugged her and said, "Don't worry, little one. I have learned to sleep sitting up. I will sleep lying down when we reach Texas. I may sleep a week."

The twins turned to him with looks of alarm on their faces. "A whole week?" Hosea asked. "I will have to be quiet a whole week?"

Sara and her father laughed at Hosea's distress in thinking his father really meant to sleep a whole week. "I will place you in school and then sleep," Adan promised. This did not make Hosea happy.

"School?" Hosea turned to his twin. "School for us?"

"Yes," Ester said. "You will not like school, but I will."

Sara and Adan laughed when Hosea said, "I will not go to school at all in Texas."

"Do not worry, my son. You will like school in Texas." Adan tousled his frowning son's hair. "You will like everything in Texas."

Sara knew her father was trying to comfort Hosea, but she was not sure she would like everything in the States. *Will I make friends with the Anglos? Will the boys and girls make fun of me because I do not know English? And my clothes? Will they suit?* Her bottom lip began to quiver at the thought of so many things she would have to face in the future. But Ronaldo left no time for her to spend worrying.

"Come! Let us be on our way," he urged.

Adan handed the rolled tortillas with beans to Sara. "Keep these in a safe place until suppertime. Try to sleep now, for I will need your help tonight to watch for bandits on the highway." Sara knew the bandits were harassing travelers even on the main roads. There had even been some killings. The Mexican highway police in their green rescue cars had doubled their patrols, but still there was some danger.

Even though the twins were now clean and rested, they began bickering. Sara knew it was time for her to make up new stories for them. This kept them occupied until they tired from listening. When the twins settled down for their naps, so did Sara.

Their sleep was not sound. Ronaldo had to dodge the many potholes on the busy Pan-American highway. Worse than the swinging and swaying of the truck was having the paved highway stop at the edge of each village they passed through. The dust would swirl around them as the truck rocked and rolled over the hard, rutted village streets. The highway pavement began at the outskirts of each village.

The bandits did not wait until dark. On a lonely stretch of the road, a pickup truck and a black sedan pulled out from behind some roadside bushes and surrounded Ronaldo's truck. His abrupt braking woke Sara and the children. When Sara realized what was happening, she pushed the twins back down on their mats. "Be very quiet. Don't move."

Chapter Two

Sara stared at the bandit who came to the rear of the truck. He waved a wicked-looking pistol in her face. "Give me food!"

She offered him the rolled tortillas. He snatched at them. "Be still and you won't get hurt!" he ordered before he rejoined his two companions at the side of the truck. One of the men was holding a rifle on Adan. The other one was shoving Ronaldo.

"Give me your money, man. You must have money if you are going to Texas!"

Ronaldo pleaded with the bandit. "We are poor. We have nothing of value." The bandit cursed and hit Ronaldo on the side of his head with the rifle butt. Sara saw it happen. She was peeping through the side window of the camper shell. It was all she could do to keep from screaming. Blood from the blow ran down the side of Ronaldo's face as he lay on the ground. She could hear Lupe softly weeping.

"Get that woman out of the truck. Get those

children out of the truck. You have no money. We take the truck," yelled the man with the rifle pointed at Adan. "Hurry, or you will get the same treatment that one got." He kicked at Ronaldo's ribs. The unconscious man jerked from the blow.

Sara could not let them hurt her papa. She dropped back to the truck bed and quickly loaded her rifle. She did not know if she could shoot a human, but that man was not going to hurt her papa.

She motioned for the twins to lay low and quietly crawled over the tailgate. She ducked low, as she walked around the opposite side of the truck from where the bandits stood with her papa. The bandits had their backs to the truck. Adan, seeing his daughter, backed away toward the highway ditch.

She raised her rifle to brace it on the hood of the truck. "Look at me!" she shouted and pointed her rifle at the man holding his rifle. At the sound of her voice, both men swung around. Adan dived at the man with the pistol. Lupe pulled the iron skillet from behind the seat and swung it at the third man. He tried to duck, but Lupe's skillet caught him on the side of his head. Down he went. Adan and the other bandit rolled in the dust of the ditch.

"I have not killed any children, yet," growled the bandit with the rifle. "If you do not lower your rifle, I will certainly shoot you."

Sara waited no longer. She squeezed the trigger, aiming at the shoulder of the arm holding the rifle. She did not miss. She was a good shot, and it was close range. In the forest she had killed several snakes, a young jaguar, and a charging wild boar on the forest trail.

The man screamed, dropped his rifle, and

grabbed at his bleeding shoulder. Lupe, for all her ungainly build, picked up the bandit's rifle and yelled, "Adan! Turn him loose. Let me kill him!"

There was no further need for shooting. The man wrestling Adan gave up. "No, please, no! Do not shoot," he begged.

Adan quickly tied the man's hands with a rope Ronaldo had placed in the truck. He also tied up the unconscious man Lupe had hit with the skillet. The man with the wounded shoulder was sitting near the ditch screaming curses as Sara held her rifle pointed at him. The twins, unnaturally silent, crouched behind the truck in peeking distance from the action.

"I will tie your hands in front of you because of the pain," Adan said to the wounded man. The man continued to curse, but sat very still while Adan tied his hands.

Lupe was busy trying to revive Ronaldo. She poured their drinking water all over his head. "Ronaldo, speak to me," she pleaded.

Adan, his prisoners all secured, walked over and took the water bottle from Lupe. "How can he speak if he drowns?" Sara laughed at her father's teasing. Even as she laughed, she began to weep.

"Oh, Papa. What if—"

"But you did not, Sara." He took the rifle from her and placed it on the seat of the truck. Then he pulled her into his arms and began comforting her. "You saved us, my daughter. You were very brave." She continued to weep. The twins came and huddled about her, patting her, urging her not to cry.

"He's alive!" Lupe shouted. She sat with Ronaldo's bruised head against her breast. "He spoke!"

"Turn him loose, Lupe. Let me see his head," Adan said. He examined Ronaldo's head wound. "He is lucky. The place is beginning to swell."

"Lucky?" Lupe moaned.

"Yes. The swelling is coming to the outside. There will be no pressure on his brain. Remember Nicko, the sawyer? When the limb fell on him, there was no outside swelling of his head. He died two days later."

Lupe nodded her head that she remembered.

Ronaldo, who had opened his eyes and was listening, groaned. "I think my head is cracked. It hurts so bad. It hurts to look." He made an effort to move away from his wife. She continued to hold him.

"No, Ronaldo. Be still. Adan has not told us what we are to do with the bandits."

Ronaldo had a puzzled look on his face. "Bandits?"

Adan laughed. "So, you cannot remember?" He pointed over to the ditch where the bandits sat huddled together. He pointed, "That one hit you with his rifle."

"But, but ... how did you capture them?" He turned from the sight of the men and placed his hand over his eyes. "The light hurts. I think we must find a doctor for me," he groaned.

"We find a policeman, first," Adan said.

"But how?" Lupe was helping Ronaldo to his feet.

"Do you think you can drive the car, Lupe?" Adan pointed to the black sedan with the black glass windows. "If you can, you can take Ronaldo and the twins and follow me to the next town. Sara will ride with me."

"But Papa, what about them?" Sara waved her hand in the direction of the prisoners.

"Take your rifle and aim it at them. I will put them in the back of the camper and lock the door." Adan raised his voice. "You can watch them through the little window. If they do not behave, we will stop and I will shoot them." Sara gasped before realizing her papa was bluffing. But she knew the bandits did not know her papa was a kind and gentle man. Yet, he would do what was necessary to protect them. She lifted her rifle in easy firing position and followed her father as he herded the men toward the back of the truck.

The first village they came to did not have a sheriff or a jail. The lone policeman on duty told Adan to take the bandits to the next town. "In that town there is a sheriff and a jail and a hospital, too." He patted Sara on the shoulder and said, "You are a very brave girl." He checked the lock on the camper before waving them on their way.

Lupe was not a very good driver, but luckily she had no accident before she parked the car behind Ronaldo's truck in the next town. Soon after Adan went into the sheriff's office, Ronaldo's truck was surrounded by policemen.

In a little while, Adan helped the twins from the car. He told them, "Sara and I have to stay to make a statement about the attempted robbery. You will stay with us and be very quiet." He helped Ronaldo from the car and placed him in the truck. "Lupe," Adan said, "the policeman is taking the wounded bandit to the hospital. You must drive the truck and follow the police car."

Sara listened while he gave his statement to the sheriff. Then, holding tightly to his hand, she told how she had decided to shoot the bandits if she had to. "They hurt Ronaldo. I thought they might kill my papa."

"You might have killed someone else." The sheriff seemed surprised she had not. "You are lucky you hit him in the shoulder."

"But that is where I aimed. My father taught me how to shoot. It was a long way through the forest to my school."

Adan smiled and explained. "There was no one to walk with her. She insisted on going to school down in the village." He hugged her shoulders, then added, "She is a good shot. There is a bobcat and a jaguar hide back at the house to prove it. And," he hooked his thumbs in his belt and leaned back, "this is the skin of the smallest snake to confront her." The men standing around listening to their story bragged on her. Sara was proud. But more than proud, she was tired and very sleepy.

Her father must have understood, but he shook his head sadly. "We cannot afford to go to a hotel, Sara. But," he turned to the officers, "perhaps you will permit us to sleep tonight on the benches." He gestured toward the waiting room.

The sheriff shook his head. "No." Then he smiled and said, "We would be ungrateful not to offer you and yours a free night's lodging." He said to one of his men, "Javier, take them to the hotel. Tell the manager to send the bill to my office."

Sara sighed and smiled her thanks and reached for her rifle. At first the sheriff refused to give it to her.

"But it is mine!"

"They will take it away from you at the border."
When the officer saw the look of distress come

16

across her face, he smiled. "All right, take it. I will write a letter to the chief inspector telling him you are very careful—a real heroine." He handed her the rifle.

When the policeman explained about the Beltrans needing a room and why, the manager of the hotel was very nice to them. He sent up fresh orange juice for them. First, Adan bathed, for he was going to the hospital to check on Ronaldo and Lupe. While he dressed, the twins bathed. When he was ready to leave the room, he said to Sara, "Keep the door locked. Do not let anyone inside but me."

Sara checked the lock twice before she bathed. Her mind was so tired that she forgot to say her prayers or hear the prayers of the twins. She fell into the bed and was at once asleep.

Sara woke only once that night to let her father into the room. She asked no questions, but went back to bed and fell asleep. She awoke the next morning to hear Adan scolding the twins. "Be quiet. Your sister is a heroine. She needs her rest. It is not every day a twelve-year-old girl will shoot a man to save our lives."

Sara wanted to laugh out loud. *Me? A heroine? If they only knew how frightened I was. If they knew how close I came to not pulling that trigger.* Then she remembered the wounded man. She sat up and asked, "Papa! Is he dead?"

"Who? Ronaldo? Of course not."

"The bandit. The one I shot. There was a lot of blood."

"Yes, I know." Her father walked over to the bed. "He will live to be in jail a long time. The authorities have been looking for him and his men for several months."

17

Sara sighed. "I am glad he did not die. I would not want to ever kill a man."

Her father laughed and pulled at her braid. "Then it is lucky you hit him where you did."

"It is where I aimed."

After they had eaten breakfast, Adan told them they would be leaving soon after lunch. "We will have an extra passenger."

"Who?" they asked.

"Lupe, because of the excitement, went into labor last night. She and Ronaldo have a baby boy."

"But how can we travel so soon?" Sara remembered her mother had stayed in bed several days after the twins were born.

"The doctor said if Lupe will rest on the trip, it will be all right." Adan smiled and reached over to smooth the frown from his daughter's face. "The doctor also said the baby is very healthy and will eat and sleep all the way to Houston, Texas."

The first day Lupe and the baby slept all day in the back of the truck. Sara rode with them. The twins rode in front with Adan and Rolando. Adan drove. Rolando still had a headache, but he was proud of his son and did not complain much.

Toward evening, they neared a church campground that the church maintained for travelers. "We will be welcome to spend the night here," Adan said.

The nuns were excited about the newborn child. "Please name him Maria," pleaded one of the nuns when she heard they had not decided on a name. "Surely the mother of Jesus was watching over you."

Ronaldo finally decided. "We will name him Francis Adan Maria Beltran, in honor of my father and my uncle, Adan."

18

The next morning, with fresh food supplies bought from the nuns, they continued their trip through Mexico. Again, Adan drove. Ronaldo promised to drive later on that evening when it was cooler.

Now as they neared border towns, there was more traffic on the highway. "Less danger of having to capture more bandits." Adan looked over at Sara and winked. She knew he was very proud of her.

Sara remembered what her grandmother had said when she had complained about not getting to go to a better school. "No matter how bad things are, Sara, if you turn it over to the good Lord, something good will come out of it." *Yes*, Sara thought, *we must always trust the Lord.*

Lupe and the baby still slept a lot. He was often hungry and Sara was no longer embarrassed at seeing Lupe feed him. She was learning that sometimes one had to forget what was "nice and proper." What was important was getting to Texas.

Chapter Three

Adan and Ronaldo had all the papers ready when they reached the Mexico-Texas border at Matamoros. Even so, it took a long time to be checked through customs. When Sara began to complain about being hot and tired, her father said, "We are fortunate to be citizens of the United States. Some have to wait days or weeks for clearance. Some do not wait, but try to cross the border illegally. They have to run and hide from the immigration officers. They are always afraid they will be caught and returned to this country. Some pay much money to crooks for false papers and then are caught and have to return to their country."

Sara thought about what her father said. She would not like to have to be afraid all the time. She remembered being afraid in the forest. It was a bad feeling. Yet, there was a difference, she knew. *I knew I would soon reach school or home. Those people can never be unafraid unless they go back to their country and get permission to enter the United States.*

The baby kept crying. Lupe was getting cross, too. The twins were running around the waiting room trying to see what everyone there was doing. Finally, Adan and Ronaldo came back with the necessary papers.

"Sara," Adan said, "they have taken your rifle." She looked at him, and he shook his head sadly. "I am sorry."

"It is their rule," Ronaldo said. "Let us go. We will eat on the other side of the Rio Grande."

To Sara, the Rio Grande looked just like any other river. Even though she knew they had the proper papers, she held her breath while they crossed the sluggish river, afraid they might be stopped.

To her surprise, the Texas side looked just like the Mexico side. *Why do countries have to be separate? Why should people need birth certificates, green cards or visas? Why can we not come and go as we please? Why all the rules?* Sara wondered.

Sara did not think it fair that fences and rivers and walls should keep people bound to one country or the other. Suddenly, Sara was afraid once more. Really frightened. Not of being caught and sent back to Honduras, but of what faced them all: new school, new friends, new jobs for her father and Ronaldo. And, most important of all, could she learn English?

Chapter Four

Adan and Ronaldo laughed as they lowered the tailgate of the truck. They had traveled down several narrow streets of Brownsville before Ronaldo pulled into the parking lot near the tall, golden arches. "McDonald's!" he said. "Now, you children can eat at McDonald's." When Sara and the twins had complained about having mostly tortillas, cheese, and beans to eat on the trip, Ronaldo had promised them their first meal would be at McDonald's. Now, they were here. The twins immediately begged to be allowed to go to the playground.

"If Sara comes with us," the twins pleaded.

"First, we will order a meal," Adan said. He led them inside the brightly painted restaurant. The girls at the counter were mostly Hispanic. The problem was getting the children to make up their minds. After ordering hamburgers, French fries, and Cokes, they went to a large corner booth that would seat all of them. But the twins could hardly eat for watching the children outside in the playground.

Lupe said, "Eat your lunch. While I bathe the baby in the restroom, you may play outside." Sara liked that idea, but she did not like Lupe saying it. *I'm the boss of the twins, not Lupe. When we get to our uncle's house, will I no longer be in charge?* She slowly chewed on a French fry as she thought about that. For over six months she had been the one to see to their clothes, cook their meals, and make them behave. Suppose her aunt punished the twins. They did need punishing some of the time.

"Papa," she began, then decided she would ask him later.

"What is it?" he asked.

"It is nothing. I must hurry and finish so I can go watch Ester and Hosea."

Her father nodded, then touched her shoulder. "We must start calling him 'Joe' now that we are in Texas. It will be easier for him." Another change, Sara thought. She thought back to the happy times before their mother died. Tears came to her eyes and she ducked her head. But not before her father saw them.

He placed his arms about her shoulders and drew her to him. "Sara, everything will be all right. I know it. You will like Texas. Just give Texas a chance."

◆ ◆ ◆

After arriving in Houston early the next day, they visited with Lupe's sister and her family. Lupe and the baby would remain in Houston until Ronaldo returned from Hensley. "In two hours I will return," Ronaldo promised Lupe.

Sara knew that Hensley, Texas, was where Uncle Frank and his family lived. They would stay with them until her father could find work.

"Hensley, Texas. Pop. 24,000," Sara read the sign. "What is Pop, Papa?"

"It means population, the number of people who live in the town."

Twenty-four thousand people? Even the city where we lived did not have that many people, Sara thought. She decided the school she would attend must be very big. She did not have long to think about that, for Ronaldo had stopped the pickup in front of a blue house.

"This is the house of my brother, Frank," her father said in answer to her unspoken question.

The house was located in an older residential area. It was a three-bedroom house. There was not much front yard, but it was freshly mown. Only Aunt Rosita was there to greet them. Uncle Frank was at his job with the utility company. Alma, their fourteen-year-old cousin, was in school. Roberto, Alma's eighteen-year-old brother, was at work, too. Sara knew there were two other older sons, but they were married and lived in Houston with their families.

Aunt Rosita was fat, almost as fat as Mrs. Ramirez, their former neighbor, Sara decided. But Aunt Rosita smiled a lot and that was good. She hugged Sara and the twins. "Come, come into the kitchen. We have refreshments." There were cookies and limeade and a pot of coffee for the men.

Ronaldo refused coffee, but took several cookies. "I have to return right away to Houston. Lupe will

24

worry if I am not there soon. Adan, I will call in a day or two to see if you have found a job." They all went outside to wave as he left.

Rosita shooed the children back into the kitchen. Ester and Joe drank their limeade, and then begged to go out in the back yard.

"But there is a dog —" Sara said.

"It is all right, Sara," her aunt said. "Pepe will not hurt them. He loves children." Sara came back from the door after watching the black and white dog greet the twins.

"When will Frank be home?" Adan asked.

"Five-thirty. It is ten miles to the plant where he works."

"When will Alma be home?" Sara asked. All she knew about her cousin was from the infrequent letters and snapshots they had received in Honduras. *Will she like me? Alma is fourteen. Sometimes older girls consider younger ones pests.*

"The school bus will be here about 4:30. Let us unpack your things before they get home. Of course," Aunt Rosita sighed, "that could be midnight for Roberto."

"He works at night?" Adan asked before taking another cookie.

"He has no schedule, that one. But it is not all work that keeps him out late at night." She shook her head and a look of sadness came over her broad face. "He drives a 'hot shot' truck. That means whenever a company needs something in a hurry, they call the boss of Roberto. The boss finds what they need and has Roberto deliver it at once."

"Is it his own truck?" Adan was interested.

"No, the truck belongs to the company, but Roberto keeps it all the time. Sometimes he has to go get something at a company and deliver it to another company. *Ay mi!* He is a wild one. Now, we must begin the unpacking."

Aunt Rosita decided Adan and Joe would sleep on the double bed in Roberto's room. Roberto would sleep on the single bed. Roberto's closet was filled, so Aunt Rosita had Adan put his and Joe's clothes in a tall dresser.

In Alma's room, Sara and Ester's clothes also went into a dresser. Sara wished she had time to secretly examine all of Alma's clothes. But she would have to wait and ask Alma to show her what girls were wearing in Texas. She looked at her worn jeans and pullover and sighed. *Surely, Papa will find work and we can have more clothes.* Sara was to sleep with Ester on the double bed and Alma would sleep on the single bed.

"Aunt Rosita, did you buy the single beds just because we were coming?"

"No, Sara. Those beds have been here a long time. I bought them when my mother lived with us. The two double beds were in the boys' room. The two single beds were in here. One for Alma and one for my mother."

"Your mother is —"

"In San Antonio with my sister. It is her year to keep her. Next year it will be my brother's time. We take turns keeping our mother." Sara was pleased that the mother of Aunt Rosita had a place to stay and was not dead. She saw Aunt Rosita was looking over her clothes and those of Ester. "We will go to the resale shop and get you some more clothes when your father has a job."

"Resale shop?"

"Yes. People take their clothes that are still

26

good and sell them to the store. The store resells them. There are many good bargains there. See, Alma's closet is filled with bargains." She moved to the closet and began bringing out hangers of clothes. There were several church dresses, some jeans, some shorts.

"Do they wear shorts to school in Texas?"

Aunt Rosita laughed. "No, not in Hensley's school. But in the summer, Alma wears them. Perhaps she will let you wear some of hers until you can buy some of your own." They heard the screech of bus brakes. "We will ask her. Here is her bus."

Chapter Five

Sara stood at the window and watched several boys and girls step off the bus. She did not know which one was her cousin. The girls had turned their backs to the house and were talking with two boys. One boy appeared Hispanic, but the other one was different. He was short and slender and lighter skinned than the Hispanic boy. But he did not look like an Anglo. "Aunt Rosita, which one is Alma?"

Aunt Rosita came to the window. "The one in the blue blouse. The others are her friends."

Sara wanted to ask about the boy with the light skin, but was afraid to, since Aunt Rosita might tease her. In a few minutes Alma came through the screen door, slamming it behind her. She turned to fling her books on the couch. It was then she saw Sara standing by the window. Alma whirled in her mother's direction. She almost snarled her disappointment. "She's here! And I guess the others came, too." She did not wait to greet Sara, but ran down the hall and into her bedroom. Another door slammed.

Aunt Rosita looked at Sara and sadly shook her head. "That one just does not understand. Be patient with her, Sara. She was born here, and she does not know how hard things are now in Honduras." She hugged Sara. "She will be all right once she gets to know you and your family."

Sara did not answer. *What should I say? I wish I was back on the mountainside. Maybe Papa will not find the new job. Maybe he, too, will not want to stay here where we are not wanted.*

But Uncle Frank and Aunt Rosita seem to want us, Sara decided later when they were all at the large kitchen table having supper. Uncle Frank was laughing and talking about the good times he and her father had had when they first came to Texas. Aunt Rosita kept pushing more food toward the Beltrans as though they had not eaten the past six days.

Finally, Alma really looked at Sara when Adan told of how Sara had helped capture the bandits. Sara stared back. *Alma must make the first move to be friendly. I do not need her. I will manage by myself.* Such determination brought a frown to her face. Adan, as usual, noticed her distress.

"Sara, tonight we will sleep once more in a real bed. I believe you should get the twins ready for bed as soon as possible. Then all of us can get a good night's rest."

Joe and Ester immediately began howling to watch television.

"No, you will go to bed," their father said with a smile.

"As soon as I help with the dishes," Sara said.

"No, Sara. Alma does the supper dishes. It is our way. I cook the supper and she cleans the kitchen."

Sara forced herself to turn and speak to the sulking girl. "I will help you."

"I don't need any help from you." Alma flung her fork to the table and pushed back her chair. "Call me when you are ready for me to work," she said to her mother.

Uncle Frank looked at his brother. "That one is still angry you have come, Adan. Pay no attention to her. She has had her own way too long. But," he shrugged, "she is the only girl. We have made a pet of her."

Adan looked at Sara. There was a pleading look on his face. "Sara will make a good friend for Alma. You will see." Sara looked at her uncle and smiled. She knew it would be hard, but she would try for the sake of her father.

◆ ◆ ◆

Sara pretended to be asleep when Alma finally came into the bedroom. Alma turned on the overhead light and then began slamming drawers shut as she prepared for bed. She flicked on her radio and Ester began to stir in her sleep. Sara placed her hand over Ester's exposed ear and pulled her closer. Alma, noting Sara's protectiveness, grinned slyly as if to say, "This is only the beginning."

The next morning, Sara and Ester were up and dressed before Alma. Aunt Rosita greeted them with a hug and a smile when they came into the kitchen. "It is good you are early risers. That way there will be no trouble with the bathroom. That Alma takes a very long time to get ready."

"Will we go to school today?"

"No. Today we have to go to the health center and get health cards for the school."

"We have the health cards from home," Sara said.

"Yes, I know. But here, there are more cards to fill out."

"Will we have to have the shots again?"

"Shots?" Ester and Joe cried. Their aunt laughed at their agonized expressions.

"I do not know. But," she tweaked Joe's nose as she spoke, "you will be very brave. Are not the Beltrans capturers of bandits?" Her teasing seem to settle the children. They began to eat the breakfast she had prepared for them.

Sara and the twins played with Pepe in the backyard until the school bus came for Alma. When Sara returned to their bedroom, she was dismayed. Alma's clothes were scattered over her bed and chair. Some of them were even on the floor. Her bed was unmade. Alma's wet towel lay crumpled on the bathroom floor. Sara began to straighten the room. Aunt Rosita came to the door just as Sara hung up the wet towel.

"A miracle!" she laughed. "It is the first time I have seen this room clean and straight." She went over to Sara and hugged her. "But, I know it was not the good Lord above who performed this miracle. Sara," her voice grew serious. "You will not wait on that lazy daughter of mine. You will take care of your bed and clothes and Ester's clothes. You will make your father's bed and take care of his and Joe's clothes. That is all. Oh," she paused and grinned at the silent, big-eyed girl, "we have a washing machine and dryer in the utility room. Washing clothes in Texas, it is nothing."

31

"But the cooking, the sweeping and mopping...?"

"I will do the cooking. Alma will vacuum once a week. The mopping Alma and I will do when necessary. You will be busy watching over your brother and sister."

"But, I can do more —" Sara tried to say.

"You will be busy learning English and trying to do your homework. And," Rosita added, cheerfully hugging Sara, "learning to enjoy living in Texas."

"Aunt Rosita, have you always lived in Texas? Your Spanish is so good."

"Yes, I was born in Texas. But my mother and father never learned to speak English. All my brothers and sisters speak Spanish as well as English."

◆ ◆ ◆

Aunt Rosita's car, a late-model green Ford, was one of the first to park at the Jenkins County Health Center. Sara had been to clinics in Honduras, but none that sparkled and shone so clean as this one. There were several women with small babies already occupying the waiting room. Aunt Rosita showed the receptionist the health cards for Sara, Joe, and Ester. The woman, a Hispanic, spoke briefly with Aunt Rosita and made some notes before telling her to take a number from the hook and be seated. "We will be number four to see the doctor," Aunt Rosita explained. "It is more fair this way. First come, first served."

Joe and Ester sat in front of the clinic's television watching a cartoon. Sara tried to watch it from where she sat with her aunt, but she could not keep her mind on the program. *Suppose there is something wrong with me. Will they send me back to*

32

Honduras? What if something is wrong with one of the twins? Thinking of separating the twins brought her near panic. *No, they could not separate the twins. I will return with them to our house on the mountainside.* She began to worry. *Have we come this far just to have to return? How can we return? The bus?* Such depressing thoughts raced round and round in her head. She was surprised when Aunt Rosita pulled on her arm.

"Come, Sara. Come Joe and Ester. It is our time." Sara looked toward the door. A nurse stood there with a clipboard in her hand. With the reluctant twins in tow, Sara followed her aunt into an office down the hall. There, in swift but kindly fashion, all three were weighed, measured, and checked over by the nurse. The doctor came in and looked over their charts.

After a moment, the doctor turned to Sara and said, "I see your tuberculin test was positive the last time you were checked in Honduras." Aunt Rosita quickly translated. Sara nodded. She understood about the tuberculin test. The test had been given at the village school by the missionary doctor right before they left for Texas. "Did you have an X-ray at that time?" Again Aunt Rosita translated. Sara shook her head. The doctor then asked, "Did they give you pills to take once every day for a year?" When Sara understood what the doctor had asked, she shook her head.

"More than likely she has converted," he said to the nurse. "But we had better have an X-ray." Sara wondered why the doctor did not ask about Joe and Ester, but turned and left the room.

The nurse explained that Sara would have the X-ray that afternoon at 3:00. Then she proceeded to give Joe and Ester their tuberculin test. Joe screamed and Ester just laughed at him. "It does not hurt. See, my bubble is larger than yours." He brushed the beginning of tears from his face with the back of his hand. He studied the tiny bit of raised skin on his arm.

"Mrs. Beltran, the technician comes only in the afternoons. Can you bring Sara back at 3:00?" The nurse was marking the twins' charts as she spoke.

"Yes, I will. When will we know the results of the twins' tests and the X-ray?"

"Friday. Come back Friday morning like you did today." Aunt Rosita led the children from the office and down the hall to another office. "Here we will pay," she said. She handed the clerk the papers the nurse had given her before they left her office. Sara and the children were very quiet as they waited to see how much money it would cost for the tests. Aunt Rosita explained their father had no job, and that they had arrived in Texas the day before.

The clerk looked at the children and shook her head sadly. "I hope he finds work. Until he does, you do not owe money for our services." With this she smiled, reached into the desk drawer and brought out three pieces of candy for the children. As they left the building, Aunt Rosita explained that they owed no money because Adan had no job. When he went to work, they would pay some money if they needed to come to the clinic. *This is good*, thought Sara. *But I hope we will be paying people soon.*

Alma was in the kitchen eating cookies when Aunt Rosita and the children came back from the clinic that afternoon.

When Sara saw Alma was in the kitchen, she

34

went in to speak to her. Alma left without speaking and went into the bedroom. *Will Alma ever want to be friends?* It seemed Alma did not want to be friendly, or even nice to Sara. She came storming back into the kitchen and shook her finger at Sara. "Who told you to hang up my clothes? I don't want you touching anything of mine. Mama just told me you had to have a chest X-ray. You might have tuberculosis. You keep your germs to yourself! And stay out of my closet. I hate a snoop!"

"That will be enough of that!" Aunt Rosita arrived in time to hear the ugly things her daughter was saying. "What a way to talk to your cousin! I'm ashamed for you, Alma Marie."

"It's all right, Aunt Rosita. I know she hates it because we have come," began Sara.

"Why shouldn't I? Now, none of my girlfriends can sleep over. I guess I'll have to start taking you everywhere I go, too. Why did you have to come?" Alma's question ended in a wail and she was crying. Rosita took her by the shoulder and marched her to the other bathroom.

Sara went into the bedroom. She sat on the bed with hands folded between her knees. Her shoulders slumped. Silent tears made their way down her young face. *Yes, why did we have to come?* She kicked off her shoes and curled into a knot on the bed as she buried her face into the pillow. She longed for her mother. She missed her grandmother. She even longed for the one-room school on the mountainside many, many miles away. She did not hear her aunt enter the room. But when the bed sagged beside her, Sara sat up and pushed back against the headboard. Before she could make up a story about why she was crying, her aunt spoke.

35

"Sara, I am so sorry. Alma is not all bad. I do not understand why she is being so hateful to you. I guess the young people do not feel so strongly about helping kin when they need help. Her father must speak to her."

"Oh, no! I do not want her to be in trouble, Aunt Rosita."

"She has to learn. We may have to help others. There is so much trouble in Central America. Who knows who will be needing our help in the future."

"Maybe this week Papa will find work and we will have a place of our own."

"Let us hope so. But until he does, my house is your house. You know that."

Sara hugged the understanding woman. "You are nice," she hiccupped.

"Of course." Her aunt smiled and said, "Now, wash your face. Your father must not see your distress. It is hard on the men when they cannot provide for their families. Be tough. Alma will behave. I promise."

But will she? Sara did not believe Alma would change.

◆ ◆ ◆

Alma did not speak to Sara or the twins at supper that evening. She paused in her eating several times to speak to Roberto in English. He would laugh and wink at Sara, who, of course, did not understand a word. *Alma must be talking about me,* decided Sara. Finally, Uncle Frank spoke. "Alma, as long as we have guests at my table who do not speak English, you will speak Spanish. And," he said with a firm voice, "you will not say such things about

Sara." Sara was afraid to look at Alma. *Now, Alma will really be angry with me.*

On Friday Sara, the twins, and Aunt Rosita returned to the clinic for the results of the X-ray and the tuberculin tests. The twins showed "negative." Healed scars showed on Sara's X-ray. The doctor assured Sara she no longer had tuberculosis. "You must take one of these pills every day for a year," he said. "They will help keep up your immunity."

"Can she start to school?" Aunt Rosita asked.

"Oh, yes. She's in fine shape. And so are these two." He smiled as he led the inquisitive twins out of his office.

Chapter Six

The twins clung to Sara's skirt as she followed Aunt Rosita into the attendance office of Foster Elementary School. "Please be seated," the secretary said. Sara waited for her aunt to translate what the secretary was saying.

"You and the twins sit over there," Aunt Rosita said as she pointed toward chairs lined against the wall. The twins refused to sit, but leaned against their sister in her chair. Aunt Rosita and the secretary talked for what seemed a long time. They looked at the health records and Sara's school records.

Their aunt sighed heavily when the secretary seemed satisfied with the records. Aunt Rosita turned to Sara and said, "You will have to be in the fourth grade, since you do not know English."

"But I was in the sixth!"

"I know. It is the rule here." Aunt Rosita wiped

her face with her handkerchief. "Do not cause any trouble, Sara. A rule is a rule. And, anyway, you will ride the same bus as the twins. You will be here to see to them if there is trouble."

Sara hung her head for a moment. She did not understand why being in the fourth grade would help her learn English better than being in the sixth grade. Then she remembered what her father had asked. "Be brave, Sarita." She thought about the jaguar she had killed. She thought about the snakes she had killed. She thought about how she had helped capture the bandits. She had been brave, then. *But why is there a need to be brave in school?* She shrugged her shoulders and forced a smile to her face. Aunt Rosita patted her on the back.

"You are a good girl, Sara. Everything will be fine. You will see." She stood and motioned to the twins to follow her and the secretary. "We will take Ester and Joe to their room."

"Please," Sara whispered to the twins. "Turn me loose or we will fall."

The secretary smiled at Sara's Spanish and shook her head in despair. "I wish I knew Spanish."

Rosita smiled and shrugged. "Those three need English, not Spanish."

"They have no English at all?"

"That is right, but the twins will learn quickly. For her," she motioned to Sara, "it will be harder. But she is a good student." Before the secretary could comment, they were standing at the door to the kindergarten room. Joe and Ester peered from behind Sara's skirt as they followed their aunt and the secretary into the large room.

The young, slender, blonde teacher came to meet them with a smile on her face. She spoke to the secretary who handed her the registration cards. She smiled at Aunt Rosita and Sara before dropping to one knee beside the twins. Her light blue eyes sparkled as she greeted them in Spanish. "Hello! Are you starting our school today?"

Neither twin spoke. Sara, embarrassed by their shyness, introduced them. "This is Ester and Joe Beltran. I am Sara, their sister. We are from Honduras."

"I am Miss Holmes, and I am glad to meet you." She stood and offered them her hands. "Will you come with me? I will show you where your table is." The twins did not take her hands. They did not move.

"Ester! Joe!" Aunt Rosita urged.

"Please show us the table." Sara now had a child's hand in each of hers. "I will walk with them." She followed the teacher to the far side of the large room. Sara was practically dragging her little brother and sister. "Shame on you," she hissed at their show of reluctance. But neither would sit down. Big, silent tears began to slide down their pleading faces. *Ay mi!* Sara thought. *Now I will have to stay with them.* Miss Holmes must have sensed Sara's thought, for she put her arms about the pair.

"We are getting ready to have chocolate milk and crackers. Please sit down and eat with us."

"See?" Sara laughed. "School will be fun." The twins had pulled out their chairs and were now seated at the table. "I will be here to get you this afternoon when school is over," Sara promised.

The teacher looked at their registration cards. "There is no need for you to come. I will place them on the right bus." She turned to Sara. "It is better this way. You will see them on the bus." Sara could say nothing. She did not want to argue with the teacher.

Sara handed the twins their lunch boxes and whispered, "Be brave. Papa will be proud if you are brave." For a moment she was afraid her reference to their father might bring tears, but the twins straightened in their chairs and grinned. Sara shook her head at them. "Be brave, not monkeys."

Miss Holmes went to her desk. She handed Aunt Rosita a sheet of paper. "This is the list of supplies the twins will need," she said.

◆ ◆ ◆

"Now, we will enroll *you*," Aunt Rosita said as they returned to the school office.

The secretary had Sara's papers ready. "Come with me," said the secretary. Sara lagged behind her aunt and the secretary as they walked to the far side of the building. "This is the fourth-grade wing," said the secretary. Aunt Rosita nodded and explained to Sara. There were four fourth-grade rooms. Sara was taken to the last one. Sara now knew exactly how the twins had felt.

The secretary knocked on the door and the teacher came out into the hall. "Mrs. Dinkins, this is Mrs. Beltran and her niece, Sara Beltran. She will be in your class." Sara waited for her aunt to translate. But Aunt Rosita was busy talking to the teacher. Sara looked at the woman and wondered what kind of teacher she would be. Mrs. Dinkins was older than the kindergarten teacher. Her hair was brown and gray and cut short. She wore glasses, and did not wear high heels. Instead, she wore walking shoes. She had on a dress. The kindergarten teacher had had on jeans. *Maybe it is a rule that if you are old you wear a dress.* Sara knew there must be a lot of rules for her to learn. She was glad she could wear jeans, for she had no pretty dresses. Aunt Rosita had not taken her to the resale shop.

Finally, Aunt Rosita finished speaking to the teacher. "Sara," Aunt Rosita said, "this is Mrs. Dinkins. She will be your homeroom teacher. Tomorrow, you will start English lessons. The first period you will go to Room 103. Then you will come to this room. See, it is Room 121."

"Does Mrs. Dinkins speak Spanish?"

"No, Sara, she does not. But you will soon learn enough English. Now, I have to go." She gave Sara a hug and left. Sara stood very still. She stared at the floor. She was afraid to look up at the teacher. Then she felt a hand on her arm. It was a gentle touch. Sara looked at Mrs. Dinkins. The teacher was smiling.

Mrs. Dinkins said, "Sara?"

"*Sí.*"

"Come with me." Sara frowned. What had the teacher said? Mrs. Dinkins smiled again and pulled on Sara's arm and opened the door. Sara went through the door and then stopped. Twenty-two pairs of eyes were staring at her. Her heart began to beat so fast she thought she might explode.

Mrs. Dinkins began to speak to the children. "This is Sara Beltran. She is from Honduras. She does not speak any English. We must be kind and help her all we can." Sara heard her name. She knew Mrs. Dinkins was talking about her. *What is she saying?* Before she could wonder more, Mrs. Dinkins took her arm and led her to an empty desk and motioned for Sara to sit down. Sara sat down

42

and stared at her desk. All the children were watching her. She could feel the red rising up her throat and face. She kept staring at the desk.

Mrs. Dinkins returned to her desk. "Children, we will continue with our math lesson." It was then she noticed that Sara had not brought a notebook or pencil. "Sara," she said, "come here." She motioned for Sara to come to her desk. Sara slid out of the chair and walked slowly forward. Mrs. Dinkins opened her desk drawer and pulled out two sheets of paper and a pencil. She handed these and a textbook to Sara. "Page 23," she said.

"*Gracias*," whispered Sara. She returned to her seat and wondered what "page 23" meant. She looked at the girl sitting next to her. The girl leaned over and opened Sara's book to the correct page. The page was filled with fraction problems to be solved. This she knew how to do. She began to write the answers. At the bottom of the page was a written problem. She tried and tried to determine what the words asked. Finally, she folded her hands and sat quietly as she waited for the class to be over. Tomorrow, she promised herself, she would bring her Spanish/English dictionary.

When the bell rang, the children stood and gathered their papers and books. Sara stood, too, wondering what was to happen now. She wanted to follow the talking, laughing boys and girls out of the room. Yet, she did not know where to go. Mrs. Dinkins, who had finally noticed Sara was standing at her desk, called to Sara. "Why, Sara. I'm so sorry I forgot about you. You've been so quiet. It's lunch time. Wait here," she motioned. "I'll get Mrs. Carrasco." Sara only understood Mrs. Dinkin's hand motions. She knew she was supposed to wait.

43

Mrs. Carrasco, the aide, came bustling into the room in a few minutes. She was a short, stout woman with black hair and eyes that sparkled. "Oh, you poor child," she said as she came to where Sara was standing. The wonderful part was that she said it in Spanish. Sara felt like crying. "Did you bring your lunch or will you eat in the cafeteria?"

"I have money. I will eat in the cafeteria."

"Fine. I have a class this period. I cannot go with you." She frowned as she spoke. "But you will be all right." She took Sara's arm and led her out into the wide hall. "Just go down this hall, turn to the left, and it is the last door on the left. There is a sign." The tardy bell sounded and Mrs. Carrasco hurried down the hall toward her classroom.

Sara was almost afraid to leave Room 121. But she was hungry. First, though, she had to go to the bathroom. *Where can it be?* She turned left and began walking toward the end of the hall. Next to the sign that said "Cafeteria" were two solid wooden doors. The sign on the first solid wooden door read "Boys' Restroom." The sign on the second solid wooden door read "Girls' Restroom." Sara did not know what either sign meant. *What had Aunt Rosita called it? I should have written down that word and placed it in my purse.* Just then the second wooden door swung open and two giggling girls came out. Sara caught a glimpse of the interior. She sighed heavily. *Yes, this is the one.* She stared at the sign on the door. "Girls" she whispered. She did not know she pronounced it "Guls."

She slipped inside and could not believe the row of stalls. *With doors, too. Such privacy!* When it came time to wash her hands, Sara stood back, for there were two girls already at the wash basins.

Both turned and looked at her, then at each other, and shrugged. They did not speak. Sara stared at the floor until the girls left.

Her stomach growled and she knew it was time for another new experience. The cafeteria. Several boys and girls were still in line when she entered the cafeteria. *Good!* she thought. *I can watch them and then do what they do.* Two of them bought sandwiches, and the third boy bought a plate lunch. "$1.10" read the sign by the steam table. Sara quickly counted her money. Sara had $1.25, enough for the plate lunch. It had spaghetti, corn, and a fruit salad. She took a glass of milk. The tax kept her from buying ice cream. She was glad her father had taught her about the U.S. money during the nights she had sat with him as they drove toward Texas. They had also practiced the English alphabet. Adan did not know it all, but he taught her what he remembered. "The 'J' is the hardest. 'H' is bad, also," he had said. But he had not told her words that started with either letter.

Sara watched the other children. They seemed to be hurrying through the meal. She did not know when the bell would ring. She saw that they returned their trays to a large window where a woman waited inside the kitchen to take them. Sara, too, hurried, for now only two or three teachers and four children were in the cafeteria. But where would she go after she took her tray to the big window? Luckily, the bell rang just as Sara placed her tray in the window. All she knew to do then was to return to Room 121.

Mrs. Dinkins gave her two more textbooks and a list of supplies she would have to buy before the next day. At the top of the page was "Wal-Mart."

Mrs. Dinkins asked Linda, the girl sitting next to Sara, to show Sara what the list contained. Linda showed Sara the things that were on the list.

Six folders	One map pencil
One pencil pouch	Notebook and paper
Two pencils	Two bottles of glue
One box of crayons	Two spiral notebooks
Two red checking pencils	A pencil sharpener

I wonder if Papa has enough money to buy me a backpack, too? At the end of that period, Sara followed the children into another room. That teacher's name was Miss Showern. She was the art teacher. She had a list of supplies to buy, too. Then they had a recess, only they called it "P.E." They ran relays. Sara was very fast, but no one seemed to care.

Sara then followed the students to Room 120. This was the science room, but Sara did not know that. The teacher, Mrs. Smith, smiled, but could not speak Spanish. She gave Sara another textbook. When the bell rang, the children returned to Room 121. Mrs. Dinkins gave them magazines to read. When the final bell rang, she handed Sara a slip with Bus No. 56 written on it.

"Jeff," Mrs. Dinkins said. "Take Sara to Bus No. 56. She will get off the bus at your stop." Sara only recognized the number "56" on the paper. When the black boy came to her and motioned for her to follow him, she did. They walked down the hall and out the side doors to where the buses were lined up. Sara had to hurry to keep up with Jeff, who, of course, knew where he was going.

Before she saw the number on the bus, Sara heard two familiar voices shouting "Sara! Sara! We are here!" She began to run toward the bus. A hand reached out and pulled her to a stop. She looked up into the eyes of Mr. Elam, the principal.

Mr. Elam said, "You know better. No running allowed!" His voice was harsh. *What is he going to do to me?* Before she had an answer to her unspoken question, she heard the voice of Mrs. Carrasco.

"Oh, Sara, you must not run to the buses." Then, in English, she explained to the principal that this was Sara's first day and that she was not familiar with the rules.

"Then tell her," the principal said before he turned and left. Sara decided right then that she would learn all the rules as soon as she could. Mrs. Carrasco led Sara to Bus No. 56 and explained the rules.

"Sara, no running to the buses, or running inside the school building. Someone might get hurt. Do not walk between the buses or across the driveway. If there is a problem, go speak to the bus monitor." She pointed to a woman teacher standing by the entrance to the school. "When you get on the bus you must find your seat and stay seated until it is time for you to get off." She looked down at the puzzled girl. "You do know when to get off the bus and where you will catch it in the morning?"

Sara shook her head. "No." She wondered where the boy, Jeff, had gone. She handed Mrs. Carrasco the slip of paper with "Bus No. 56" written on it.

Mrs. Carrasco followed Sara onto the bus. She spoke to the driver. Joe and Ester kept calling for Sara to come sit with them. Finally, Mrs. Carrasco yelled, "Quiet, please." The children on the bus became silent. "Who is to tell Sara when she is to get off the bus?"

At the back of the bus a voice called "I will."

"Who said that?" Mrs. Carrasco began walking toward the rear of the bus.

Jeff stood up. "I did. She gets off at my stop."

"Make sure she does," Mrs. Carrasco threatened. She left the bus and Sara hastened to squeeze in with the twins. They were excited about their first day at school. Sara finally had to hush them so she could watch the route of the bus. She wanted to count the blocks, but had waited too late to start. *In the morning, I will count them and try to learn the route. What if we missed the bus? Could we walk to school?*

When they had made several stops, Jeff came up and touched her on the shoulder. He motioned with his head that it was time for them to get off the bus. They stood on the curb until the bus pulled away. Jeff pointed down the street to the blue painted house.

"*Gracias*," Sara said.

Jeff shrugged. "It's okay." He turned to leave, then pointed at the departing bus, and then at where they stood. "Seven-thirty." He frowned, then grinned. "*Mañana.*"

Sara laughed. Jeff was the first student who had tried to speak to her. "*Mañana*," she replied. "Seven-thirty." She would remember to ask Aunt Rosita what "seven-thirty" meant.

Chapter Seven

Sara kept waking up during the night, thinking that it was time to get ready for school. Aunt Rosita had promised she would have the children all up and ready in time to catch the bus at 7:30. Still, Sara was afraid she might oversleep. When she heard her aunt in the kitchen making coffee, she hurried to dress.

"You are an early riser," Aunt Rosita said. "But, today, that is good. We need to talk."

"Is something wrong?"

"No, not yet." Aunt Rosita poured herself a cup of coffee and leaned against the cabinet. "After everyone went to bed last night, a policeman came looking for Roberto."

"He is in trouble with the law?"

"No, I don't think so. Not with the police. I think there will be trouble with his father tonight."

"Is there something wrong with Uncle Frank?" Sara's voice showed her fear.

Aunt Rosita put her cup down and began to laugh. Finally, she said, "I said it all wrong. There is nothing wrong with your Uncle Frank. But when he discovers what the policeman told me, there will be something wrong with Roberto."

"What do you mean?" Sara came closer to her aunt. "Is it a secret?"

"No, no secret. Roberto was out last night with two of his friends. After he left them, the boys robbed a pizza parlor."

"Oh, Aunt Rosita! Why did the policeman come looking for Roberto?"

"To make certain he was home and wasn't the one who drove the getaway pickup truck."

"Was he?" Sara hated to ask, but she wanted to know.

"Yes, for once, he was home. His boss had told him to stay by the telephone, for he was expecting a rush job for Roberto." Aunt Rosita began frying the sausage for breakfast.

"Then what is the problem?" Sara began buttering the bread for toast.

"I do not want you or the twins to hear your Uncle Frank tear into Roberto for being with thieves. The policeman said it was not the first time Roberto's friends had been in trouble."

"Oh, Aunt Rosita, did Roberto know?"

"I am afraid so. After supper I want you to ask your father to take you and the twins to the park. You do not need to be here when your uncle gets angry." She smiled, then became serious once more. "And I want Frank to be angry. Roberto has to learn to choose his friends more wisely."

As Sara set the table for breakfast, she wondered about the friends she would make. When she had lived in the city in Honduras, her best friend had been Nora Perez. She wondered what Nora was doing. *Probably getting ready for school, just like me.*

Alma did not ride the same bus as Sara and the twins. Her bus came earlier at 7:15. Alma rushed into the kitchen and grabbed a piece of toast. "I'm late," she said to her mother, who was begging her to sit down and at least eat some cereal.

"You wouldn't be late ..." Aunt Rosita began. But Alma was already at the front door.

"Don't forget, Mama," she called back over her shoulder. "You promised to take me to look for my dress."

So, Alma is to get a new dress. She has a closet full of dresses. Sara did not speak her thoughts. The night before she had asked her father when she could have more clothes for herself and the twins.

"As soon as I get my first real paycheck, Sarita." Sara did not beg. She knew he would do as he promised.

◆ ◆ ◆

Room 103 was near the fourth-grade wing. Sara had no trouble finding it. She was to learn to speak English in this room. She wished they had left Honduras earlier. It was hard starting in the third week of school. The teacher in this class spoke Spanish as well as the kindergarten teacher had. Sara was so relieved. She issued Sara a textbook that had the initials ESL on the front. Beneath them was the name of the book: ENGLISH AS A SEC-OND LANGUAGE. Then she saw that there were other non-English speaking students in the room besides the Hispanics. Several were Asians, and two appeared to be Hispanic, but they spoke a very different language. She discovered later that they were from Saudi Arabia. Because the teacher could work only with a few students at a time, Sara knew learning English would be very difficult. She spoke to the boy next to her and immediately the teacher called her name. "Sara. In here, we speak only English. Do not speak Spanish. If you want to say something to me or to a student, look up the words in your dictionary."

Sara ducked her head. She knew she was blushing. The boy across from her touched her arm and grinned. "It is okay," he said in English. Then he quickly wrote what he had said on a slip of paper and handed it to her. He pointed to her dictionary and then to the note. She straightened in her chair and smiled at him. Maybe he would be her friend.

This is the class that will mean the most to me. Here, we are all equal. We are fighting the same battle—to learn English. She realized they, too, would be making mistakes. No one would make fun of her efforts. She would not criticize their efforts. She even felt very sorry for the Asians, for they did not have the same alphabet.

When the bell rang, Sara went immediately to Room 121. The math lesson was very easy. The rest of the periods were spent trying to translate with the aid of her dictionary. It was very boring. Several times she would take out her ESL book and try to at least learn the words.

When the final bell rang, Jeff came over to her desk and motioned for her to follow him. "Bus," he said.

"*Sí*. Bus." Only it came out "boose." She would have to practice that at home.

◆ ◆ ◆

After supper Adan took the children to the park. He had quickly agreed to Sara's request when she whispered, "We must talk." While the twins were swinging, she explained why she had asked him to take them to the park.

His face grew solemn. "I did not know. But I did know you would not have asked me if it had not been important."

"What do you think Uncle Frank will do to Roberto?" She remembered stories of other family quarrels.

"I do not know. Frank has a temper. He is very proud of his position with the utility company. He is a hard worker. The other boys did not give him this kind of trouble."

"Will Roberto listen?"

"Oh, yes," Her father smiled and said, "Frank weighs more than Roberto." Then his voice grew serious. "Yes, Frank will see to it that Roberto listens." When they returned to the house, Roberto was nowhere to be seen. Alma was at the kitchen table doing her homework. Adan and the twins joined Uncle Frank and Aunt Rosita in the living room to watch television. Sara went to her room and opened her ESL book. *If Alma would only help me.* She whispered the consonants, but she knew she was not saying them correctly. Then she tried the things she had learned that morning in class. "Hello. How are you? My name is Sara."

"Hello," Roberto spoke from the doorway. "I'm

fine. How are you?" Sara giggled with her cousin. He came in and squatted on the floor by the bed.

"You will learn. But you have to practice," he said in Spanish.

"Was it hard for you?"

"No. We spoke Spanish and English at home. Mama made us. By the time I was in kindergarten, I knew English. Now, I am afraid I will lose my Spanish. I seldom use it."

"You have no Hispanic friends?"

"Oh, yes. But mostly they are newcomers and want to practice their English."

"Like me." She slid off the bed and down to the floor beside him. "Would you say these for me?" She showed him the word list for the next day.

"My pleasure. Do you think you can learn to speak English in two weeks?" His face grew serious and the twinkle disappeared from his eyes.

"Why in just two weeks?"

"Papa said I will have to stay home each evening for two weeks." He shrugged, but did not smile. "I will be glad for your company."

She touched his hand. "Roberto, I am glad you were not with your two friends."

"I am, too."

"But you are eighteen. You have finished school. Is your papa still the boss of you?"

"As long as I am under his roof, I do as he says. It is our rule." He shrugged and pushed back against the wall. "One day I will be my own boss." He took her ESL book and began her lesson.

◆ ◆ ◆

When the weekend came, Roberto was still

54

grounded. He had been faithful in helping Sara each evening with English. Alma had protested the second night. "Why don't you come and play cards with me?"

"When Sara learns English, she can play with you."

Sara said nothing until Alma left them. "That one slams doors very often."

Roberto laughed and pulled on Sara's braid. "That one has her nose out of joint." Then he had to explain that expression to Sara.

Saturday morning Sara changed the beds and swept the two bedrooms. She cleaned the bathroom, too. Then, she gathered up their dirty clothes. Aunt Rosita showed her how to operate the washer and dryer. She folded the clothes and put them away in the chest of drawers. Roberto got up at dawn to mow the grass. When he had finished that, he began washing his truck and his father's truck. Sara went outside and offered to wash Aunt Rosita's car.

"No," her father said. He had a bucket of water and a sponge in his hand. "As soon as Roberto is finished with Frank's truck, I will wash Rosita's car." Sara knew her father was bored. Each day he had been going to the employment office to look for work. He would go stand on a street corner with other unemployed men. Sometimes contractors would drive up in their pickup trucks and hire one or several men to go out on a job for a day. Adan had worked two days of the week. But he needed a regular job. Sara prayed each night that her father would find work.

That afternoon Adan said she could take the twins to the park. "Come home in time for supper," he said. There was a wading pool for little children in the park. Ester and Joe would play in the water for hours. Aunt Rosita fixed a juice bottle with limeade and ice for them to take. Sara placed several paper cups in the large brown sack with her ESL book and note pad.

"If I remember how my children acted, you will need more than one cup each," Aunt Rosita said. The twins carried towels and Sara had the brown bag and her books. She was glad the park was only two blocks from the house.

◆ ◆ ◆

Sara pulled one of the park benches under a tree where she could sit in the shade and watch the twins. They knew not to run on the wet concrete around the pool. Several other children were already in the pool. Nearby, under another tree, sat a girl who appeared to be several years older than Sara. Sara tried not to stare, but she could see the girl was crying. *Why?* Sara pulled out her ESL book and note pad and began to write the spelling list. After thirty minutes, Joe came running up to dry his face.

"We have friends, Sara. We have new friends!" He turned and called, "Ana! Ciro! Ester! You want limeade?" Ester led two younger children out of the pool to where Sara was sitting. They appeared shy, but approached Sara as she watched them come across the grass. Suddenly, the girl Sara had noticed stood up and began walking toward her also. She was taller than Sara, and darker skinned. Her hair was loose about her shoulders. *She's pretty*, Sara thought. *But why is she coming over here?*

Chapter Eight

Sara waited until the older girl arrived. By then, Ester had told her the older girl was the sister of their new friends. She knew not to offer the limeade to Ciro and Ana without the girl's permission.

"Hello," Sara said.

"Hello," the newcomer answered in Spanish. "Are my brother and sister bothering you?" She placed her hands on their shoulders.

"Not at all. I wonder if they can have some limeade. We have plenty." Sara pulled the large bottle of limeade from the brown bag. Ester began to pass out the cups. Sara said, "Wait, Ester . . ."

"They would love to have some limeade and so would I," the girl quickly answered. "My name is Anadelia Perez. This is . . ."

"Ciro and Ana. I already told her," interrupted Joe.

Sara looked up from pouring the limeade and

57

smiled. "And that rude little boy is Joe. His twin is Ester. I am their sister. I am Sara Beltran."

"It is so good to hear Spanish," Anadelia said as she and Sara drank their limeade. The children had finished and were now headed for the swings.

"I know. We have been here only a week. We are from Honduras."

"We came during the middle of August. We are from El Salvador." The girls began to exchange experiences. First, they talked about the trip to Texas. "We came by airplane. I was so frightened," Anadelia said. "It was my first trip."

"How long did it take?" Sara had never known anyone who had flown on an airplane.

"A little over three hours."

"*Ay mi!* We were six days arriving here." Sara shook her head in disbelief that Anadelia had come farther than they in such a short time. "I would have been very frightened of flying in an airplane. But, then," she grinned at her new friend, "I was very frightened when the bandits came."

"Bandits! Were you attacked by bandits?"

"Well, yes," Sara began, wanting to be truthful. "They did stop us. And I guess Ronaldo was attacked." She went on to tell about that experience.

"You were very brave. Imagine, you learned how to shoot when you were just nine years old."

"It was not my choice, Anadelia. My papa said I would have to learn or not go to school. The forest trail was too dangerous without a rifle."

"I am not brave. If my father's life was not in danger, I would move back to El Salvador and live with my grandmother."

Sara wanted to ask about Anadelia's father, but decided to wait. She knew it was not good to know

58

some things. Instead, she asked, "You are afraid here in Texas?"

"I am unhappy here." She paused and Sara could see the tears clouding Anadelia's eyes. "I hate school. In El Salvador I was in the seventh grade. They have placed me in the fifth just because I do not know English."

"Do you go to Foster Elementary School?"

"Yes, and I am with those babies. I am fourteen years old."

Sara did not like being called "a baby," but she understood. "I was in the sixth grade in Honduras. Now, they have placed me in the fourth. I am eleven, almost twelve years old."

Anadelia put her arm about Sara. "Oh, Sara. I did not mean you were a baby. I am sorry." She began to cry. "I am the baby. I wish, I wish, oh, what is the use to wish?"

Just then the twins and Ciro and Ana came running up to the girls. "We're going back into the pool," Joe shouted without waiting for Sara to give them permission.

Sara turned to her friend. "They are not unhappy. See, Anadelia, how lucky they are. They are not wishing. Memories do not bother them."

"Ana is five and Ciro is four years old. They do not know what it is to be afraid." She told how her father, a professor, had to be smuggled out of El Salvador. "The enemy soldiers came at night to search our house."

"Did they hurt any of your family?"

"No. The father of my mother is a very important man."

"Has your father found work?"

"Oh, yes. He is teaching at the college. We are safe here. Has your father found work?"

"No, Anadelia. Not a regular job. Just a day or two at a time. But Uncle Frank is trying to get his company to hire Papa."

"Has your mother found work?"

"My mother is dead. We are staying with Uncle Frank and Aunt Rosita." She pointed down the street to the blue house. "Where are you living?"

"We live in the apartments over there." Anadelia pointed to the apartment complex across from the park. The girls continued to talk until Sara realized it was time to return home.

"We must go." She wanted to ask Anadelia to come visit her, but first she knew she must speak to Aunt Rosita. After all, it was her house.

Anadelia called to her brother and sister. "It is time for us to go, too. Will you be here tomorrow afternoon?"

Sara smiled. *So Anadelia is going to be my friend.* "Yes. Will you be here?"

"We usually come around 4:30. I will look for you."

◆ ◆ ◆

That evening at the supper table, Sara told about meeting Anadelia, Ciro, and Ana. Alma looked at Sara and frowned. "She is fourteen and in the fifth grade? She must be stupid."

"Alma!" Aunt Rosita slapped her daughter's hand. "It is the rule. She probably does not know English."

"Would you like to go to the park with me tomorrow afternoon and meet her?" *Why did I say that? If Alma does go, she will probably be ugly to Anadelia.*

60

"Not me. I am going to the baseball game with Wanda."

"We want to go to the baseball game, too. Ester?" Joe looked at his twin.

"No. I want to go to the park to see Ana. She is my new friend."

"She is my friend, too," Joe said.

"No, she is a girl. You can be friends with Ciro."

"He is only four years old," Joe complained.

"Four and a half, he said," Ester said with a smirk on her face.

Adan stopped talking to Frank long enough to say, "Joe, you and Ester hush and eat your supper. I imagine both the Perez children will be your friends."

Roberto had been listening to the conversation, too. "Sara, this friend of yours, is she pretty?"

"Yes. She is tall and slender and . . ."

"Is fourteen years old," Aunt Rosita finished. "Behave yourself, Roberto. Maria Hernandez is more your age."

"And weighs twenty pounds more than me," he grumbled.

"In two weeks she may weigh less," his father reminded him. Sara hid her grin behind her napkin. Roberto had ten more days of being grounded. "Hell" he had called it. Sara had learned to say the word in English. *Why is it so easy to learn the bad words first?* Her father had given her an angry stare the first and only time he heard her say it.

◆ ◆ ◆

Sunday afternoon Sara and the twins headed for the park. This time they had money for snow cones. The man with the snow cone machine only

61

came on Sundays. Anadelia was at the bench under the big tree. The children were in the pool. Sara waited until Joe and Ester joined them. She took their clothing and towels and walked to the bench where Anadelia was sitting.

"I am so glad you could come," Anadelia said. "Mama and Papa are sleeping. I had no one to talk to."

"Have you made a friend at school?"

"No," was her sullen reply. "I do not want to be friends with the Anglos."

"Why not?" Sara wanted to make friends with everyone.

"There is one in my math class who makes fun of me."

"But all Anglos are not like that." Sara felt sorry for Anadelia. Sara remembered Linda had been kind to her. And Jeff—but he was black. Was he an Anglo? She would have to ask Papa. "Who is this girl who makes fun of you?"

"Her name is Patsy. She is a leader in the class."

"How can you tell if you do not speak English?"

"Oh, Sara. One can always tell who is a leader. The other students cluster around her. Sometimes they bring her candy or cookies." Anadelia nodded her head emphatically. "I was a leader in my class back home. I know."

Sara thought for a moment about the one-room school back on the mountainside. Then she smiled at her friend. "At my school there were no leaders." She began to tell about the village school. "Four first-graders, two second-graders, one third-grader, five fourth-graders, no fifth-graders, and me, a sixth-grader."

"Is that all? How many teachers?"

"Just one. The parish priest. Sometimes the missionary lady from the city would teach us geography. The priest said he could not keep up with the changing countries or their names."

"Were there any boys in the school?"

"Only in the winter. The village is a poor one. The boys have to work the fields. In the wintertime, the missionary lady comes more often. The priest is old and cannot stay warm enough in our building."

"That must have been very hard for you. Did it snow?"

"Sometimes, a little. But then we had fun." Sara did not want to talk anymore about the village school. She wanted to know about Foster Elementary. "Who is your teacher?"

"He is Mr. Elam. I do not like him, either. He is very stern." Anadelia stood and pulled at Sara. "Let us walk around. Maybe we can see some boys."

Chapter Nine

Sara and Anadelia had the same lunch period. Mrs. Carrasco had asked Mr. Elam, the principal, for permission for Sara to eat at the fifth-grade table with Anadelia. Sara saw the girl named Patsy the first day she ate with her friend. Patsy was very pretty and wore makeup. Her hair was blonde and she had blue eyes. She was not as tall as Anadelia. She seemed to wear something different every day. "She mixes her clothes," Anadelia explained. "She has expensive clothes. I hear her father is the mayor of Hensley."

Patsy did not say anything to either of the girls. But each day she had something ugly to say about them or the Asians sitting at the fourth-grade table. Sara could tell by the snickering among Patsy's friends, and the sly looks Patsy aimed at them. But one day, the day before Halloween, Patsy made the mistake of not seeing Mrs. Carrasco was in hearing distance of the fifth-grade table.

"My daddy says they should load all the Hispanics into cattle cars and ship them back across the border." Her friends laughed. Then she said, "They certainly wouldn't notice the smell in the cars."

"Patsy Trumble, watch your trashmouth!" Mrs. Carrasco ordered. Patsy whirled about and faced the irate aide. Sara could tell that the girl was not frightened, for she merely shrugged and returned to her meal. *What has she said this time?*

One of the bilingual fourth-graders whispered, "I hope they expel her."

"They will do nothing to her. Her father is the mayor," Anadelia said. "My father came up to speak to the principal about Patsy. But the principal said he could do nothing unless there was a fight."

"What did Patsy say?" Anadelia asked the fourth-grader.

"She said that her daddy said he wished they would ship all the Hispanics back across the border in cattle cars. That we would not notice the smell in the cars."

"Would not notice the smell?" Sara was slowly rising from her chair. Mrs. Carrasco was across the room speaking to Mr. Elam. Patsy and her friends were still whispering. They did not seem to be intimidated by what Mrs. Carrasco had said.

The fourth-grader nodded. "Yes, that means she thinks we stink."

"Stinks?" Sara carefully laid down her fork. How dare Patsy say such a thing! Sara remembered her father telling her not to cause any trouble. He knew she sometimes lost her temper. "I'm sorry, Papa," she whispered. "No one is going to say I stink and get by with it."

Walking slowly toward the serving line, Sara

saw that a tall glass of strawberry Kool-Aid cost twenty-five cents. She had twenty-five cents. No one was going to say that she "stunk." Placing the icy red drink on a tray, she walked slowly between the fourth-grade tables and the fifth-grade table where Patsy sat.

"*Ay mi!*" Sara cried, as she stumbled before reaching Patsy's chair. The glass of bright red Kool-Aid went sailing off the tray, throwing its contents all over the back of Patsy's white shirt and white jeans. Patsy screamed and rose, sending her chair back against the chair of a fourth-grader, causing him to spill his milk all over the table in front of him. When Patsy turned and saw it was Sara who had had the "accident," she was furious.

"You did that on purpose, you, you ..." She sputtered to a stop at the fake look of contrition on Sara's face.

"I am so sorry," Sara said in Spanish. "I will go for a mop." She turned right into Mr. Elam, who had witnessed the whole thing. Mrs. Carrasco was right behind him.

"Did you see what that dirty girl did to me?" Patsy's face was almost as red as the Kool-Aid. "What are you going to do about it?" Sara could not believe a student would speak to the principal in that tone of voice.

"Why, Patsy, I'm going to help Sara mop up this mess. It was just an accident. You may go get some clothes out of the PTA clothes closet."

"I won't wear poor people's clothes! I'm going to call my mother." She did not wait for permission, but stormed by the unsmiling principal.

Sara stared mutely at Mrs. Carrasco. *Will they expel me?* she wondered. But Mr. Elam had said it was an accident. She finally had nerve enough to look up into the tall man's face. She saw the corner of his mouth twitch as though he was trying to keep from smiling. And wonder of wonders, he winked at Mrs. Carrasco. "Lilly, do you think you and Sara can clean up this mess?"

Mrs. Carrasco laughed. "It will be a pleasure." She put her arm about Sara and led her back toward the kitchen. "Such a lovely accident, Sara. But now we will have to clean up the mess."

"I know. But I can do it by myself. I made the mess."

"But Mr. Elam and I enjoyed watching you do it."

"He is not angry?"

"No, Sara. The mayor is as bad as his daughter."

"Why does the principal not make her stop talking so ugly about Anadelia?"

"Sara, principals can only do so much. There are many rules." She led Sara to the cupboard where the mops and paper towels were stored. Sara took two rolls of towels from the shelf. Mrs. Carrasco filled the mop bucket with soapy water. Anadelia met them at the kitchen door.

"I will help, too," she said as they returned to the site of Sara's revenge. The students at the fourth-grade table moved their chairs back so the girls could wipe up the spilled milk.

"Mrs. Carrasco, will you tell that boy I will bring money for the milk tomorrow." Sara looked at the boy as she said that. Mrs. Carrasco repeated what she had said in English.

"There's no need of that," Mr. Elam said. He walked up to the table where the boy sat and put his hand on the boy's shoulder. He said, "Go get another glass of milk. And get an ice cream, too." A broad grin split his usual solemn face. "It's for wear and tear on your nerves." All the children at the fourth-grade table laughed. Sara dared not look at the students at the fifth-grade table. She did not know what Mr. Elam had said. Neither did she understand when he patted her shoulder and said, "Spunky. I like spunky girls."

◆ ◆ ◆

Sara wanted so badly to tell her father what she had done. Yet, she knew it would worry him. He wanted her to get along with her fellow students—to cause no trouble. She did not know what Patsy would do the next day.

After supper there was a knock on the door. Sara was in her room studying English with Roberto. He was waiting on a call from his boss. She did not hear the knock, but she did look up from her ESL book when her father appeared in the doorway. "Come into the living room, Sara. We have company who wants to meet you."

Was it the mayor? Surely not a policeman. Roberto seemed to sense her fright. "Trouble at school?" he asked. He did not wait for her to answer, but took her hand and led her into the living room.

A tall, muscular, white-haired man was sitting in the recliner. He stood when Sara came into the room. "So, this is our little avenger," he said in a deep voice. He looked at Adan and smiled. "They seem to come in all sizes."

"She has not told me what you are referring to, Professor Perez." Adan looked at Sara, a questioning look on his face.

"Permit me, then, to enlighten all of you. I have had a very graphic account from my daughter, Anadelia."

Sara expelled a tremendous sigh of relief. *This is her father. He is not the mayor or a policeman.*

"Please," Aunt Rosita said, "please, everyone sit down." She began introducing her children to Mr. Perez. "We are all curious to know what Sara did. Surely she was not in a fight."

"Mr. Beltran, your daughter did not fight. She used her brains." He relaxed into the recliner and began to tell the story. First, he told how his daughter had been treated by Patsy Trumble. He then told of his visit to the principal. "Before, in our country, the principal would have punished that girl for her rudeness. There, no one is allowed to speak out on their beliefs. The soldiers are ever ready to take offense at anything. I hope Texas will not become like my country." He then began to tell what had happened in the cafeteria at lunch.

All through his recital, Sara could feel Alma's eyes on her. *What does she think about what I did?* He had to stop when he came to the part about drenching the bigoted girl. Roberto practically rolled on the floor where he was sitting. Even Alma laughed. But Adan did not laugh.

The professor turned to him, for he had noticed Adan was not sharing their amusement. "What is it? Are you afraid you will have trouble? Could the mayor revoke your green card, your right to be in Texas?"

"No. I am a naturalized citizen of twelve years. Sara was born in Texas. That is not the problem." He threw up his hands in the air. "If I had wanted to be around a fight, I would have stayed in Honduras. What will happen now to Sara? Are there not more Anglos than Hispanics at that school?"

Uncle Frank spoke. "Adan, you need not worry. I do not think the mayor will permit his daughter to continue harassing the Hispanics. He is up for election in the spring of next year."

The professor beamed. "So I have heard. And I have also heard Hispanics are beginning to register to vote in Texas. That is good. Now, I will finish my description of the incident." He went on to tell what Mr. Elam had done and said to Sara. "He said, 'Spunky. I like spunky girls.' And so do I, Sara Beltran." He stood and walked toward the door. "I wish Anadelia had half as much spunk as you." He shook hands with the men and nodded to Aunt Rosita. "I do not have time to accept your gracious offer of refreshments, for I have many essays to grade. I came to meet an exceptional young lady." He offered his hand to Sara. It was the first time in her young life that a grown-up had ever wanted to shake her hand.

"So," Roberto teased after the professor had gone and they were all seated around the kitchen table. "You continue to be the heroine. First, the bandits, then you handle the daughter of the mayor. What next?"

"Peace," Adan pleaded, but Sara could see he was proud of her.

"But not submission," Uncle Frank said as he waved his fist in the air. "But enough about this girl. I, too, am a hero today."

They all began to clamor for more information. Aunt Rosita finally said, "Hush, all of you. He is my husband. I will ask the questions." She waved her fist in her husband's face. "Not another near electrocution?"

"No. But it has to do with giving a new life to Adan."

"What are you trying to say? Make sense."

70

"Mr. Smith told me to have Adan report for work Monday morning. He will be trained as an ..." They did not let him finish. Everyone was clapping and laughing.

Finally, Adan raised his hands. "Quiet, please. I must know what I am to be trained as." He looked at his brother.

"You will be trained as an operator. You have enough English that you will be able to interpret and train others in the next few years. We are expanding and moving southward. It is a good opportunity for you."

"Yes. And I thank you for your help." Adan looked at his brother's wife. "And you, too, Rosita. You have been most patient."

"Now, they can move out Monday," Alma said, with a pleased look on her face.

"Alma, go to your room!" Her father stood and shook his finger in her face. "Immediately!" Sara saw that for once, Alma had pushed her father too far. She reached for the twins.

"The park. Let us ..."

Uncle Frank's anger disappeared. "No, Sara. You do not have to leave because of my anger. I am calm. But I am not through with that selfish daughter of mine."

Chapter Ten

A week passed before Patsy sought her revenge on, strangely enough, Anadelia. The blonde girl, surrounded by four of her friends, walked up to Anadelia, pushed her against some lockers, and slapped her face. Sara was not there, but heard about it when she went to lunch.

"Where is Anadelia?" she asked the bilingual fourth-grader at the next table.

"Haven't you heard? She got into a fight with Patsy. The principal sent both of them home." Sara went flying across the room to where Mrs. Carrasco stood talking to another aide.

Mrs. Carrasco said, "Don't run in the cafeteria, Sara. But I know what you want to know." She excused herself from her friend and led Sara out into the hall. "Yes, Anadelia was sent home. She was accused of starting a fight."

"Anadelia start a fight? No. Anadelia is a coward!"

"Perhaps she is. We believe she did not start the fight. However, four friends of Patsy said they were eyewitnesses and so testified."

"It is unfair. You know they are lying."

"Yes, and so does Mr. Elam. But all he can do is what he did. He sent both girls home for the day."

"What will happen now?" Sara made up her mind that instant that she would get even for Anadelia.

"Nothing is going to happen. Professor Perez has called the principal and he is taking Anadelia out of this school."

"Oh, Mrs. Carrasco. She is my only close friend."

"I know, Sara. But you must not get involved further. I do not want Patsy to turn on you." She led Sara back into the cafeteria. "It is better that you return to your fourth-grade table."

Sara made no attempt to hide her tears from the girls at the fifth-grade table. She stopped and stared at the four who usually accompanied Patsy. She stared a long time. She stood there not saying a word.

Then she walked to where she had placed her knapsack. From it she took a sheet of paper. She brought out her Spanish-English dictionary. It took her several minutes to search for the word. Then she was printing it in large letters on the paper. It seemed everyone in the cafeteria was watching her when she went around the fifth-grade table and held the sign that read "LIARS" over the heads of Patsy's four conspirators. The students at the fourth-grade table began to clap. Soon, everyone nearby was clapping. Mr. Elam came running over, followed by Mrs. Carrasco.

"Now, now, none of that," the principal called as

he took the sign out of her hands. He turned to Mrs. Carrasco. "Bring her to my office." He left, followed by the frightened student and the compassionate aide.

"Sit down, Sara. You, too, Mrs. Carrasco. And please make certain she understands what I am about to say." He looked at the aide. She nodded. "Sara, I know you are angry." He paused and waited for Mrs. Carrasco to interpret. "I know they are liars, but I do not have proof. It was Anadelia's word against the five of them." He leaned back into his chair and stared out the window.

"It is not fair," mumbled Sara. Mrs. Carrasco spoke to the principal.

"No, it is not fair," he said. "But I hope it is settled. Patsy has had her revenge. Perhaps she will back off and leave you alone, for Anadelia is not coming back to school."

"Why? What will she do?" Sara frowned as she waited for his answer through Mrs. Carrasco.

"Anadelia cannot adjust to Texas. Her father is making arrangements to send her to a convent in Guatemala. She will be safe there."

"Safe? Is she in danger?" Sara was up leaning over the principal's desk.

"She will be safe at the convent in Guatemala. Her father says he cannot send her back to El Salvador. The terrorists might kidnap her and hold her hostage to force him back to El Salvador."

After Mrs. Carrasco told her that, Sara moved back to her chair. She slumped, dejected. *Be brave in school? No, it is better to be a coward. What am I to do now?* As if in answer to her unspoken question, Mrs. Carrasco placed her hand on Sara's shoulder. "Sara, you will be all right. And I think you need not worry about Patsy or her friends. I believe your sign shamed them—and the students clapping like they did. I don't think Patsy will misbehave again."

"It does not matter." Sara was openly sobbing. "May I go to the restroom now?" When Mrs. Carrasco repeated Sara's request, Mr. Elam said, "Please use mine. Wash your face and then lie down on the couch until the bell rings. I will get you a tray to eat in here."

Sara stopped crying when Mrs. Carrasco told her what he had said. Her widened eyes expressed her surprise. He and Mrs. Carrasco laughed at her. Finally, Mrs. Carrasco said, "Sara, he does not want the other students to think he has been beating you. Come, we will wash away those tears."

◆ ◆ ◆

That evening, Professor Perez paid another visit to the Beltran house. This time he had time for refreshments. Alma was sleeping over at a friend's house. Roberto was out on a call. Only Aunt Rosita, Uncle Frank, Sara, and her father sat around the kitchen table. The twins were already in their beds. The professor began to explain the reason for his visit. "Did Sara tell you what happened at the school today?"

"Yes," answered Adan. "I am very sorry. I wish I could help, but I am afraid for Sara."

"It is Sara's safety I have come to talk about. I am disappointed that Mr. Elam did not believe my daughter."

"But he did!" interrupted Sara.

"I know, what I meant was that he was unable to say he believed my daughter."

"Patsy's friends ..."

"Sara, let the professor finish what he started to say. I want to know why he is concerned about your safety." Adan had his hand on her shoulder.

"Do you not believe that Trumble girl will try to harm Sara?" The professor seemed troubled as he asked.

"No, I do not think she will try anything physical. I believe her to be a cowardly bully. From what you and Sara have told us, Anadelia has never taken action against her tormentor. Sara did. Patsy will not risk another such encounter."

"What if she has her friends ...?"

"Sara tells me she shamed those friends. Tell him, Sara." Embarrassed, she looked at her father. "Tell him," he said again.

Sara did. She also told him what Mr. Elam said. She told him how Mr. Elam had brought her lunch to his office. "Mrs. Carrasco said she is going to write a letter to the editor of the *Hensley Tribune*. She said she is going to quote the mayor's daughter on what her father said about the Hispanics."

"Ah, the election." For the first time that evening the professor smiled.

"I am not worried," Sara said.

"She is very brave," Aunt Rosita said.

Professor Perez clapped his hands in his excitement. "I know! I know!" He reached for Adan's hand. "Dear friend, I wonder if you would let me send your daughter to the convent where I am sending Anadelia?" He hurried to explain. "I would pay all her expenses and give her an allowance, too. It is a very fine school. They offer many advantages. And," he smiled at Sara, "every one of them in Spanish."

Sara was speechless. She couldn't believe that

this rich, important man would be willing to send her to a great school. She looked at her father. She saw his face draw sad. She heard him sigh. *What is he thinking?*

No one spoke for a few moments. Finally, Adan straightened his shoulders and spoke. "You have honored my daughter. And you have honored me with such an offer. But I am afraid I must turn it down. I start a regular job now. The twins and I need Sara. We will soon have our own apartment."

"But, Papa . . ."

"I would help with the twins," Aunt Rosita offered.

"No, Rosita. You have reared your family. And Sara, I know this is a wonderful opportunity for you, but I need you. The twins need you. I would not want to have to trust them to a day care center. They have already lost their mother. They have been uprooted twice." He paused, looking at her disappointed face, "And most of all, Sara, I could not bear to be parted from you. You have been the little mother to our family."

As though ashamed of his decision, he pushed back from the table and rushed out the door. Sara followed him. "Papa, Papa, please wait. Don't leave. I was only thinking of the good times for me. I had no thought about you or the twins." She went up to where he was leaning against the back fence. "I must have been crazy for a moment. How could I ever think of leaving you and the twins?" He turned and swept her into his arms. He placed his wet cheek against hers. They stood like that for several moments.

Finally, he straightened and released her. In a shaky voice, he said, "Come, let us go back and tell the professor goodbye."

◆ ◆ ◆

Sara and Anadelia said their own goodbyes
Saturday afternoon in the park. Sara tried not to
show her sadness, for Anadelia was so happy and
excited about returning to Central America.
"Guatemala is not El Salvador, but it will be more
like home than this place," she said.

"But you will be far away from your family.
How will you stand it?"

"I would have been sent to a convent school
when I reached fifteen, anyway. I will fly in every
now and then to visit my parents. It only takes a few
hours. I will call on you the first time I return."

Sara again realized how different their
lifestyles were. In Texas, there were many degrees
of lifestyles. In Central America, one was either rich
or poor. "I will miss you," was all she could say to
Anadelia.

Chapter Eleven

"Thanksgiving?" Sara looked up from her ESL book without too much enthusiasm. Since Anadelia had gone, all she did was study. She still had no special friend at Foster Elementary School. "What is that? A church service?"

"Well, sort of. At least many churches hold services celebrating Thanksgiving," explained Aunt Rosita. "School will be out at Wednesday noon. And it will not start until Tuesday."

"Why?"

"Next to Christmas, it is our favorite holiday. We will celebrate with turkey and dressing . . ."

"What is that?" Sara placed her book on the table. Aunt Rosita now had her undivided attention.

"What is what?" Aunt Rosita was patting out cornmeal tortillas. "You know what a turkey is."

"Dressing. Is it like things you put on salads?"

"No, Sara. It is a mixture of cornbread, eggs,

celery, bell pepper, onions, white bread and several spices. In Texas, we favor sage."

"Do you fry it?"

"No, Sara. We stuff the turkey with it and then place the rest of the dressing around the turkey in a baking pan. Then, we bake it for a long time."

"May I help you fix it?" Sara wanted to learn all the Texas ways. What Aunt Rosita had called Tex-Mex cooking was not Spanish cooking. Nor was it food like that cooked in Honduras. But Sara liked it.

The Beltrans all went to the community Thanksgiving service in the high school auditorium Thursday night. Sara and the twins did not understand what the speakers were saying, but they enjoyed the music. And it was the first time they were in a gathering of other Hispanic families. During the refreshment time after the service, Aunt Rosita and Uncle Frank introduced Sara and her family to other Hispanic families.

"This is Mr. and Mrs. Hernandez and their daughter Rosie," Uncle Frank said right before they were ready to leave the school. Sara's face brightened, for Rosie appeared to be just her age.

Rosie must have thought the same thing, for she asked, "Sara, what grade are you in?"

Sara hated that question. She hated to admit she was in the fourth grade. "I'm in the fourth grade."

"They did it to you, too?" Rosie moved closer to Sara. "I'm in the sixth, finally. When we came up last year from Mexico, they placed me in the fourth grade, too."

"How did you get to the sixth?" Sara's heart ached with hope.

"I studied English very hard. My father would

not let me have any play time until I had mastered a certain number of English words each night."

"My cousin has been helping me. I will tell him that as soon as I master enough English I can be placed in my right grade." Then she remembered that as soon as her father received his first full month's paycheck they would be leaving the blue painted house. *Well, I can do a lot in a month*, she promised herself.

On the way home from the Thanksgiving service, Aunt Rosita explained why people in the United States of America celebrate Thanksgiving. When she had finished, Sara looked at her father. "Papa, we are very fortunate. We did not have to freeze or starve to become citizens."

"That is right, Sara. We have much to be thankful for here in Texas," her father agreed.

"Especially for washing machines and clothes dryers," Sara mumbled. The others heard her, and they laughed all the way back to the house.

Sara began to study her ESL book more than ever after Thanksgiving. Roberto continued to help her when he was home. Patsy did not bother her, nor did Patsy's friends.

Rosie had Sara over to her house the following Sunday. All Rosie wanted to talk about was the upcoming Christmas party at the community center. "And I will have a new dress. Mama is making it for me." Rosie showed Sara the dress.

"It is beautiful," Sara said as she watched her friend turn and swirl the long, full, white satin skirt.

"I will wear a red velvet bolero with this. Mama has not finished it, yet."

"Is there a dance?" Sara faintly remembered the

81

last Christmas party she had attended with her parents when they lived in the city.

"Yes, there is. Each year the Parks and Recreation Department gives the party. The money from the ticket sale will be used in the city summer recreation program." Rosie wiped her brow. "Everyone will vote for the Winter Queen and King. It is the most important affair in this city that everyone can attend. We have so much fun. And there are delicious refreshments, for every family brings cookies or a cake."

Just thinking about the Christmas party made Sara's eyes sparkle. This was to be truly a great Christmas. That night she said to her aunt, "Oh, Aunt Rosita! Will we go? Does it cost much money?"

"Yes, we will go. And no, it does not cost much money. I am certain Adan will have enough money by then for Christmas." She walked over to the table and placed her hand on Sara's open book. "What do you want for Christmas?"

"Me? I thought we might buy for the twins. I have had no thought about something for me. We will be moving into the apartment on New Year's Day." A wistful look crossed her face. Then she shook her head as if to dislodge an errant thought. "I am big. I do not need a gift at Christmas." Aunt Rosita merely smiled at her niece.

Alma was not that considerate. She came into the room with her petulant voice geared up into a whine. "Mama! When are we going to find me my dress? I will not wear the same dress I wore last year." She perched on the table and watched her mother. She said nothing to Sara.

But Sara was curious. "Will you wear the new dress to the Christmas party?"

82

Alma turned and looked at Sara. "Yes, of course." She took an apple from the bowl and began eating it. She chewed for a while, then turned once more to look at Sara. "You will have to have a dress, too, you know. Everyone dresses up."

Sara slowly closed her book and pushed back from the table. She did not look at Alma or Aunt Rosita, who was busy at the stove. She called back over her shoulder, "I'm going to take the twins for a walk. We'll go to the park."

"Dress warmly, Sara," her aunt said.

◆ ◆ ◆

Sara took turns pushing the twins in the swings. The day was warm for that time of year, but the brisk breeze made the twins' cheeks and noses glow. Sara did not notice. She was trying to convince herself that she did not want to go to the Christmas dance. She did not own a dress fit for a party. The one she did have was really too tight. It was not even a party dress. The twins had only jeans and shirts. Her father had only work clothes. And he had not even worked a full month. Tears began to slide down her cheeks. She knew she should be brave and not yearn to attend the party. *I do not want to be brave. I want to be pretty in a new dress. I want a new dress for Ester. I want a suit for Joe and one for Papa. I am tired of not having anything.* She was completely miserable. Just then Ester looked back at Sara and saw the tears.

"Why are you crying?"

Sara forced a smile to her face. "It is the wind that is making my eyes water so," she lied.

Ester smiled and said, "It is my turn, so push me."

◆ ◆ ◆

The days after Thanksgiving were the hardest Sara had experienced since coming to Foster Elementary. Christmas seemed to be on everyone's lips. There would be Christmas parties at school. Aunt Rosita had volunteered to make cookies for Sara's homeroom party. In the art class, everyone was making decorations for the school's Christmas tree. They were learning Christmas carols for the school's Christmas program. All the Hispanics at Foster Elementary were asked to sing "Silent Night" on the program. Sara was one of the twenty-three children. She let out a sigh of relief when she heard they would not have to have costumes, but would wear the school choir robes. Sara knew it was taking most of her father's money to furnish the apartment.

Sara's father had taken her shopping for used furniture for the apartment. It was stacked in the Beltrans' garage. Aunt Rosita was giving them enough dishes and utensils to start with. Then there would be groceries, linens, cleaning supplies. It made Sara's head hurt to think of all the things it took to take care of a family. Her father had assured her he would have enough money for gifts for Joe and Ester, so she did not have to worry about that. Alma still did not have the dress she wanted for the party. Aunt Rosita was out of patience with her daughter.

"One more time we will go shopping. If you do not make up your mind, you can wear what you wore last year. My mind is made up to that!" Aunt

Rosita told Alma. Sara hoped Alma would find a dress. She knew Alma would make everyone in the house unhappy if she did not get what she wanted.

It was Aunt Rosita who came in slamming the front door after the shopping trip. She fell into Uncle Frank's recliner with a sigh of exasperation. "My feet are killing me! That Alma. Well, too bad about her. She can wear her old dress. The factories have not made the dress that would please her!" Alma came in crying. She went straight to her room.

Sara knew that Alma was mean to her, but she could not help feeling sorry for her cousin. She, herself, had known disappointment many times. She remembered what her grandmother had said shortly before she died: "Sara, my child, you must be brave always. You will have many more disappointments. You have no mother to understand and comfort you. Growing up is a very hard time for a girl."

Is it hard for Alma, too? Sara had never really thought about Alma and her problems. Mostly, she had made it her business to stay out of Alma's way. *It is too bad that Aunt Rosita does not know how to sew dresses.* Suddenly, Sara remembered something very important. She went into the bedroom.

"Get out of here," sobbed Alma. "I want to be alone!" Sara said nothing. She went to the bottom drawer of the chest of drawers. The bottom drawer was where she had packed it the day they had come to Hensley. She opened the drawer and slowly lifted out the bundle wrapped in tissue paper.

"Get out!" Alma said it again before she raised up from her pillow to watch Sara. "What is that?"

Sara tried to hide her smile of anticipation. She hoped her father would not care. Anyway, it now belonged to her. It would be her decision. She slowly unwrapped the layers of tissue paper, now yellowed with age. She turned and held her mother's wedding dress up for Alma to see.

"Sara! Where ... when did you get that?"

"It was my mother's wedding dress. I think it is beautiful."

Their hatred forgotten for the moment, the two girls sat and admired the richly embroidered white dress. "It is too big for me, now," Sara said. "But if you promise to be careful with it, you may wear it to the Christmas party."

Alma was speechless for a moment. Then she asked, "You really mean it? I know it would fit me." But she made no move to touch it. *She thinks it is a trick*, thought Sara.

"If you would not mind wearing your mother's red silk crocheted stole with it, I think it would look very Christmasy."

"Sara, I do not think Adan would like anyone but you wearing the wedding dress of your mother." Aunt Rosita came through the doorway where she had been standing and listening.

"It is mine to loan or not to loan. I am certain Alma will not damage it." *I am not really*, thought Sara. *I just have to trust her.*

"Mama?" Alma pleaded.

"I do not understand why Sara wants to loan you her most precious possession after the way you have treated her. I would not if I were her." Aunt Rosita stood with her hands on her hips, frowning at her daughter. "Neither would you."

Sara did not want to hear anything more. "It is for my joy, too, Aunt Rosita. I cannot give Alma a Christmas present or in any way thank her for the use of her room. Let it be this."

Aunt Rosita still did not smile. She turned and walked toward the door where she stopped and turned back to face the waiting girls. "If Adan agrees, then Alma, you are one lucky and undeserving girl."

Sara met her father at the truck when he came in from work. She explained about the dress. "I want to do this for her, Papa. I know she has been mean. But it will give me pleasure," Sara said.

He looked at his daughter and tears of pride filled his eyes. "Sara, your mother would have been as proud of you as I am. If letting Alma use the dress is your wish, then it is my wish, too."

Foster Elementary School had never been more beautiful. The children of all grades had worked hard on their decorations. Mr. Elam and the janitors had strung lights all up and down the old, dreary halls. Every room was hung with colorful paper chains and strings of cranberries and popcorn. The twins were so excited that Aunt Rosita was afraid they might make themselves sick.

Then the day for the program came. Sara and the other Hispanics sang "Silent Night" so beautifully that Aunt Rosita and some of the other mothers were openly wiping their eyes. Then the Asians sang a song about their favorite holiday. Several Jewish children sang about celebrating Hannukah. There were small presents from the Parent-Teachers Association under the Christmas tree for every student. Everyone said it was the best Christmas party ever.

The Beltrans were leaving the party when someone called, "Mr. Beltran! Wait, please."

Chapter Twelve

"Mr. Beltran!" Sara stopped when she heard the principal call her father's name. Mr. Elam was hurrying toward them with a white envelope in his hand. "I almost forgot something very important," he said as he handed Adan the envelope. "Please do not open this until you get home and have time to think over its contents. My home telephone number is on the paper. Please call me when you have made your decision." He turned to leave, then whipped back with his hand outstretched. "Merry Christmas!" Then he was off, almost running.

Sara knew that Mr. Elam had many things to do that evening before the school could be locked up for the holidays. *Why has Mr. Elam written a letter to Papa?* Although her father did speak English, he did not know how to read and write English.

"He did not want to hurt your father's feelings," Aunt Rosita explained when they reached home. "That is why Mr. Elam told him to wait until he got home to read it." No one seemed interested in the letter except Sara. The twins were comparing gifts they had received from the kindergarten tree. Her father and her uncle were talking about their work. Aunt Rosita was making a list of things she would have to buy the next day at the supermarket.

Finally, Sara could stand it no longer. "Papa, please let Uncle Frank read the letter to us." Sara and the adults were sitting at the kitchen table drinking hot chocolate. Uncle Frank put on his reading glasses and silently read the letter. Sara thought he would never finish. When he took off his glasses and returned them to his breast pocket, he looked at Sara and smiled. "This is good news. Adan, the letter says that if Sara can learn to read, spell, and say 600 words by January 15, she will be promoted to the fifth grade for the next semester. If she does well in the fifth grade that semester, she will be promoted to the sixth grade next September. That way she will only be a year behind others her age." He waved several sheets of paper. "Here are words she must learn."

"Oh, Papa! I can do it. I have four weeks to study for the test. Aunt Rosita! Where is Roberto? I will have to tell him, too."

"Wait, Sara," Uncle Frank said. "Mr. Elam said your father will have to give his permission. Mr. Elam wants to make certain you do not make yourself sick studying. It is for your father to say." Uncle Frank and Aunt Rosita left the room. They knew Adan would want to be alone with Sara.

"Oh, Papa, please. I can do it."

"But Sara, remember, we will be moving into the apartment in two weeks. You will be very busy putting the apartment in order. You will have to take care of the twins, too. And there will be meals ..."

"Please say yes, Papa. Let me at least try." She was clinging to his arm and tears were beginning to form. She blinked rapidly. *I must not cry! He will think I am still a baby.*

Adan removed her hand from his arm. He walked over to the window and peered through the blinds as though seeking his answer in the darkness outside. He shook his head as though he could not agree to that answer. "How can you learn? I cannot help you. Roberto will be here, not at the apartment."

"Rosie might. Maybe Alma?" But Adan looked at his daughter and smiled at her suggestion.

"Alma? Do not count on that one."

"But I could try, please. Tell Mr. Elam I will try." Sara was crying unashamedly. *He just has to say yes. I want to be in the sixth grade next September.*

Adan put his arm about her and pulled her to him. "I will call him tomorrow night. We can all try, Sara. The twins and I will help you all we can."

◆ ◆ ◆

The night of the Christmas party came. Alma had never looked prettier, decided Sara. Aunt Rosita had a new blue dress that made her look taller and more slim. Roberto and Uncle Frank were wearing their best suits. For a moment Sara felt sad that she and her family were not going. The twins were not disappointed, for Aunt Rosita had let each one open a present that was under the tree for them. Adan was on the floor with them helping insert the necessary batteries into the car Joe had unwrapped.

A feeling of happiness for the twins pushed Sara's sadness away. She began to help Ester cut out the paper dolls and their clothes from the book Ester had unwrapped.

In a little while, Adan made the hot chocolate. Sara brought out the special cookies she had made just for them. For the first time since leaving the mountainside in Honduras, they were alone. Sara smiled and hugged Ester. "Oh, Papa, I love Uncle Frank and Aunt Rosita, but it will be good to have our own place."

"With no washing machine or clothes dryer?" he teased.

But even that did not make her sad. "Aunt Rosita said she would come over and show me how to use the machines that are there for all the people in the building."

She cleared the table and sent the twins in to take their baths. "Joe, you use Aunt Rosita's bathroom. Ester can use ours. That way you will get through quicker so you can watch the special Christmas programs on television."

"You, too, Sara," her father said. "Tonight you will not open that ESL book or look at that list of words."

"But, Papa ..."

"No studying tonight. This is a night we will enjoy."

Sara looked at him. Her frown turned into a smile. "Yes, Papa. I wanted to watch, but I was afraid you might think I was tired of studying." She took his hand and pulled him toward her Uncle Frank's recliner. "One day we will buy one like this for you, too." *And one day we will buy a television and a lot of things.* But she did not say that out loud.

The twins were asleep on the floor. Adan and Sara were watching Flamenco dancers perform on the Spanish language station when the other Beltrans returned from the party. The men began taking off their ties the minute they walked inside. Aunt Rosita flopped into the overstuffed chair and kicked off her new shoes. Uncle Frank and Roberto wandered into the kitchen mumbling something about "a good cup of coffee."

"*Ay mi!* My feet do hurt." Sara watched with a smile as her aunt wiggled her freed toes. *Do skinny ladies' feet hurt, too?*

"I'll set out some cookies, Aunt Rosita. You sit still." She was halfway to the kitchen when she turned to ask, "Where is Alma? Did she have a good time? When will she be home?"

"Alma is with Enrique Ramirez."

"Enrique? But . . .?"

Aunt Rosita smiled. "Yes, finally. It must have been your dress, Sara. He never noticed her before." She squirmed out of the chair and stood to her feet. "I had better go check on Frank. He will have the coffee so strong we will be awake the rest of the night."

Sara went ahead of her aunt. *Well, Aunt Rosita answered one of my questions, not two of them. Alma was with Enrique. I know she has feelings for him. And being with him means she is having a good time. But when will she be home? After all, she is only fourteen. Well, almost fifteen.*

Sara's last answer came from Uncle Frank, who was looking at his watch when she came into the kitchen. "Rosita, what time did you say she must come home?"

"They were only going to the Dairy Queen. I told Enrique to have her back here before midnight."

"Midnight! That is forty-five minutes from now."

"Listen to him. His only daughter goes out for a soda after the dance and he is having a fit." She walked over and mussed his hair. "Do not worry. Enrique will have her home on time. Remember, he may be sixteen, but he had to have the permission from his father, also."

The forty-five minutes went rapidly as Aunt Rosita and Uncle Frank talked about the party and who was there. They all watched as Alma spoke to Enrique at the door. When she finally closed the door, she turned and smiled broadly at them. Sara could tell Alma was totally happy. *Maybe it was my dress. I am sure it was. I only hope Alma remembers that.*

◆ ◆ ◆

Two days later Christmas morning arrived and the twins, of course, were the first ones up. "Oh, Sara, come and see," Ester whispered as she straddled her sister. "Put on your robe. Don't get dressed. That will take too much time."

"Bring your present in here. I want to sleep some more."

"I cannot. You will have to come see for yourself," Ester said, bouncing up and down on Sara's middle.

Sara was afraid Ester would awaken Alma. There was nothing else for her to do but pull on her robe and go look at the presents her father had bought for the twins.

Joe was on his knees unwrapping a present from Roberto. He looked up when Ester and Sara came into the room. "You have a present, too, Sara."

"She has three presents," Ester corrected. "I counted them."

Sara dropped to the floor beside Joe. Ester handed her the first one. The tag said it was from Roberto. She removed the bow and carefully unwrapped the box. Inside was a soft, white sweater. One she could wear to school or church. *Oh, Roberto, you have been so good to me already. You did not have to do this, too.* Ester pushed a larger package into her hands. It was from Aunt Rosita and Uncle Frank. In the box were two dresses. *When did Aunt Rosita have time to go to the resale shop?* Both were very stylish and similar to the ones Alma and her friends wore. The final present was a small one. It was in an inlaid wooden box about seven inches long and two inches high and wide. It contained the prayer beads of her mother. Tears flooded her eyes. *I thought they were buried with Mama.* She held them to her cheek. *This is better than the wedding dress.* She kissed the crucifix just as she had seen her mother do.

Sara had been so engrossed with her gifts she had not heard her father come up behind her. His hand rested on her head. She was on her feet in one fluid movement. Her arms went around him and she sobbed as she tried to thank him. "And I don't have a gift for you, Papa." Now her tears were for him.

"Hush, Sarita. Every day you are my gift. You never whined when I did not let you go with Anadelia. You did not complain when we could not go to the Christmas party." He took out his handkerchief and wiped her tearstained face. "And did you not promise to buy me a recliner one of these days?"

The twins had been watching their sister and

father. Joe shook his head in disbelief. "Not a recliner, Sara. First, it must be a television."

Sara and her father laughed at his selfishness.

"No television until Sara learns her words." Ester said this in a grown-up voice.

The rest of the household came into the living room one at a time. Aunt Rosita was first. Sara and the twins ran to embrace her and thank her for the gifts from her family. Uncle Frank came in and got his hugs, too. An hour later Roberto came in long enough to have breakfast. Sara did not know what to say to him. Finally, she walked up to him and whispered in his ear, "I love you." Then she kissed him on the cheek. He grabbed her in a bear hug until she squealed for him to turn her loose.

"Say 'Please, Roberto, turn me loose' in English first."

She proudly repeated the words. He knew she had studied all of them. He turned her loose with a pull on her braids.

"Mama, Papa, Uncle Adan, I have a suggestion that might help Sara. Let us from now on only speak English except in emergencies. That way Sara will have to learn not only the words but where to use them."

"Oh, Roberto! That will be too hard," Sara said.

"Roberto is right, Sara." Uncle Frank looked at his brother. Adan nodded his head.

Aunt Rosita shook her head in sympathy. "We can only try, Sara."

"That is what they do in the French class in high school," said Alma from the doorway. "You are not allowed to speak English at all."

"I do not know if I can."

"You can, Sara. We will all help. You will see,"

Alma said. Sara stared at her cousin. *Can Alma have changed? Will it last?*

"Thank you, Alma. I will need all the help I can get if I am to pass the word list test." She looked at her father and he seemed to understand. *Yes, Papa. This is a great Christmas for us.*

Chapter Thirteen

Only one week before we move! How many words can I learn in one week? Sara looked at the lists of words Mr. Elam had given her to learn for the test. The words were in alphabetical order. The daily word spelling lists in the ESL class had been hard enough for her. Now, with only one week to study before they moved to the apartment, Sara knew she would have to really concentrate.

Just then the front door opened and Roberto came into the living room. From inside his padded vest he pulled out a spiral notebook.

"Roberto! Why are you not at work?" Aunt Rosita had heard the front door open and close. She was standing in the kitchen door looking at her youngest son. "Did you get fired?"

"Oh, *Mamacita*, how you fret!" He hugged her and then turned to Sara. He said in English, "I was in the neighborhood. I thought Sara might use this

97

to help her learn the words." He handed the note-book to her. "Go through that list and pick out all the words you already know. List them on one page. Then skip two pages...."

"*Despacio*, Roberto," pleaded Sara. "*Despacio*." He grinned and pulled her toward the table. He took the sheets of paper from her and scanned the words on each page. Then, knowing some of the words she knew, he began to place a check by those words. Sara watched silently as he then began to list twenty of the words that were checked on the first page of the notebook. Then he skipped two pages before continuing to list the familiar words.

Sara said, "Yes. I understand." She pointed at the words in the notebook. Then she pointed at the two blank pages. "What is this?" She could not think of the English words to ask why he was leaving the pages blank.

He understood. He looked at the first word on the list in the notebook. "Girl," it read. He turned to the blank page and numbered the first line. Then he wrote, "The girl is pretty."

"*Sí!* I mean, yes, I understand." Now she knew he wanted her to not only to learn the word, but to use it in a sentence. *Ay mi! He expects a lot from me.* He grinned and pulled on her braids. His mother poured a cup of hot, steaming coffee for him. Sara looked at him and wondered how she would thank him properly. Then she smiled. *In English, of course.* "Thank you, Roberto. You are *muy bueno*, I mean very good to me." Aunt Rosita and Roberto laughed with Sara.

"You will do very well," Aunt Rosita said.

"You had better." Robert's voice was stern, then he winked.

Sara nodded. But how could she tell them she would miss their kindness and support very much after she, the twins, and Adan moved from the blue painted house? *I will have to learn all the words, then I will be able to tell them exactly how I feel about them and what they mean to me.*

New Year's Day was moving day. That morning, Adan, Roberto, and Uncle Frank loaded the trucks with the heavy furniture. Sara packed a big cardboard box with the twins' toys and possessions. The three satchels could not hold the clothes they had received as Christmas gifts. Another box had to be found to hold the linens and utensils and dishes Aunt Rosita was giving them to get started in the apartment.

The day before, Aunt Rosita, Alma, and Sara had gone to the resale shop to buy curtains and bedspreads. These would be hung after the furniture was placed in the apartment. The only thought that marred Sara's happiness that day was not having any time to study the words. She was halfway through, but she knew most of the words were those she had known before she received the list.

Aunt Rosita had cooked a pot of beans, rice, and a stack of tortillas for their first meal in the apartment. When Uncle Frank and his family left, Sara began to set the table for supper. "Papa!" she called. "We forgot the coffee."

He came into the kitchen and asked, "Did I hear someone speaking Spanish in here?" He frowned at her in a teasing fashion. "Surely not you?"

"Oh, Papa. It is so hard," she said in English. She began to flip through her Spanish/English dictionary for the word "supermarket." It was not there. Then she grinned at him and found the word

99

"market." She looked at him with a very smug expression on her face. "We need to go to the market tonight for coffee." She knew the big supermarket was four blocks away. The weather was cold, but it was not raining. They would all walk very fast to stay warm.

Her father patted her shoulder. "After supper, we will make a list." He pointed to the empty pantry shelves and then to his hand where he made the start of an imaginary list.

"Yes, Papa. I understand. A list." Sara wished that Roberto had never suggested they speak in English. Even though she knew it helped her, it took such a long time looking up the right words.

◆ ◆ ◆

Two days later Rosie came over to see the apartment and visit with Sara. "I did not know you could cook," she said in Spanish.

Sara shrugged, "*De nada.*" Then she showed Rosie the letter from Mr. Elam. "I must use only English until I pass the test."

Rosie nodded. "That is best, but difficult to hold ..." She paused when Sara ran to get her dictionary out of the kitchen. Rosie grinned and waited patiently for Sara to look up "difficult."

"Difficult," repeated Sara. "Yes. But you will help me?"

"Yes. The next word is 'conversation.'" For the next hour Rosie and Sara worked on the word list. The twins were busy playing with their toys and did not bother them.

Sara looked at the clock and closed the notebook. "I will make soup for supper."

"May I watch?"

Sara smiled at the older girl. *I can cook, she can speak English. Maybe we can exchange talents.* "Come, I will show you how to make soup." Before going to work that morning, Adan had cut up the fryer into boiling pieces. These Sara took from the refrigerator. She placed them in a pot with water and placed it on the electric stove. She placed a cover on it after she had added some salt, black pepper, and chopped cilantro. Next she cut two onions in fourths. She did not know the word "fourths," so she said, "Four pieces, each."

"Into fourths," prompted Rosie.

"Fourths." She peeled and sliced three carrots and six large potatoes. Each time she worked on a vegetable, she said its name in English. She sliced and chopped a bell pepper. Finally, she carefully removed a jalapeno pepper from the jar. She removed the seeds, then chopped the pepper. Then, she immediately washed her hands.

Rosie laughed at her precaution. Sara grinned, then lapsed into Spanish. "Don't laugh, Rosie. Back in Honduras the first time I cut some jalapenos for my grandmother to pickle, I did not know they could burn my hands like fire. Not all at once, but after I finished cutting them." She paused and shook her head at her own stupidity. "My hands began to glow. I had to keep them in water for several hours. Now I am very careful."

"You are speaking Spanish." Joe had come into the room unnoticed. "I am going to tell Papa on you." Sara knew the twins were very proud of how easily they were learning English words. But she had her bluff in on this one.

"And I will write to Susie White and ..."

101

"No, Sara. I will not tell Papa. Please, Sara," he begged, his face a fiery red.

Rosie giggled. "A girlfriend already?" But Joe did not stop to explain. He ran from the room. Rosie turned back to her friend the chef. "When do you put the vegetables in the pot?"

Sara looked at her friend, a frown on her face. "When do I," she pointed to herself, "do what?"

Rosie seemed to be thinking. Finally, she said. "Vegetables." She pointed at the mixing bowl of prepared vegetables. "When do you cook them?"

Sara said, "Thirty minutes. Then cook thirty minutes."

Rosie nodded. Then she said, "Let's play UNO while we wait."

Sara opened her dictionary. "UNO?" she muttered.

Rosie laughed and opened her shoulder bag. She pulled the game of cards from the bag. The next thirty minutes the girls laughed more than they played. For Rosie was faithfully trying not to speak Spanish as she taught Sara how to play UNO.

◆ ◆ ◆

When Adan came home, the soup was ready. It only took Sara a few minutes to butter and heat the flour tortillas she had made the night before. Adan asked the blessing. The twins complained that Sara had thrown away the wishbone. Adan cautioned them to speak English.

"Is there an English word for 'wishbone'?" Joe asked.

"Yes," said Adan. "There are English words for everything." Joe groaned and Ester laughed at him.

102

"And, there are English words that mean many things," Sara said slowly, making certain she was using the correct words. "Like *pass*.

Pass the football.
There is a mountain *pass*.
I may not *pass* the test.
I will *pass* by the school.
Please *pass* the tortillas."

Adan and Sara looked at each other. He reached out and patted her hand. "I know it is hard, Sarita. But you will learn."

Ester, who had been listening all the while, said, "But you are a very good cook, Sara. I know you will find a husband and cook for him. You do not need to know English to do that."

Adan hid his smile and frowned at his younger daughter. "You are so smart," he said in Spanish. "But you, like Sara, will speak in English. Do you understand?" The six-year-old nodded, but Sara could tell Ester would do just as she pleased, for it was her way.

Chapter Fourteen

Sara felt like crying. Before Christmas, she had plenty of time to study her ESL book in her other classes. But now, after being in school two days, she could not concentrate on the word list. She had learned so many new words during the holidays that she was recognizing a lot of them when the teachers spoke to the class. But she was still not able to follow the teachers' directions, or comprehend when the students took turns reading aloud. Yet, she kept recognizing words she knew. It kept her from shutting out what was going on in the class. She had so little time to learn the words now.

The next morning she arrived early and received permission to speak in Spanish to the ESL teacher. "I thought when I agreed to study for the word test that I would have the same amount of time as before."

"Well, is there not the same amount of time?"

the ESL teacher asked as a frown creased her forehead.

Sara tried to explain. "Before I learned so many English words, I could shut out the class and the teacher. Only in math could I participate, since numbers were used instead of words." She sighed. A forlorn look swept across her usual placid face. "Now, I keep hearing words I know and I look up and then I listen for some more and then ..." Tears filled her eyes. "Oh, Mrs. Welch, I do need more time to study."

Mrs. Welch put her arm about the distraught girl. "I understand, Sara. But the rule is that before we can get state money for your attendance, you have to take certain subjects."

"Even if I do not understand what is being said?"

"That is correct. It sounds stupid, I know. But it is the rule. Do you study at home?"

"Yes. But first I must clean the bathroom and the kitchen. Then decide what to cook for supper. Then, if there is washing and drying to be done, I have to do that. Papa is working long hours now."

"Does your mother work? Do you have to do all that by yourself?"

"My mother is dead. This is my work. I have been doing it ever since my grandmother died ten months ago." Sara said it as if she wondered why the teacher had even asked. "When Papa does not work overtime, he helps me. The twins are beginning to help. They make up the beds. They will be seven in April."

"You are really very special, Sara Beltran," whispered the teacher. "I shall speak with Mr. Elam. Perhaps we can see that you have more time to study. You are very bright, you know." The bell rang and Sara went to her desk. She felt better for having talked with Mrs. Welch. *But can she and Mr. Elam really do anything to help me? There are so many rules.*

The next morning Mrs. Welch called Sara to her desk. "I have good news for you, Sara. Mr. Elam contacted a language volunteer. She will meet you in the cafeteria right after the last lunch period. You and she will work on your word list." She stopped and smiled at the look of joy on Sara's face. "Yes, Sara. You are going to make it. You really are."

Sara came into the cafeteria after the last lunch group left. Her heart was beating very fast. *I hope the language volunteer will like me. I hope she does not think I am stupid.*

Sara stopped. *There she is. It has to be her. There is no other person in the cafeteria. But she is a teacher?* The woman did not look like a teacher. She looked like Sara's grandmother had looked before she became ill. She was short, fat, with gray hair braided and wrapped around her head. She wore glasses, and she had on a black dress with a shawl about her shoulders. *She looks Hispanic*, thought Sara. *But can she speak English? No, this must be some child's grandmother, not a teacher.* Sara waited. Perhaps another lady would be there soon to teach her.

"Sara?" called the lady. "Sara, please come over here." Sara could do nothing but go to the lady. *She will waste my time.* But Sara was reared to be polite.

"Hello," she said. "Are you the language volunteer?"

"Yes. I will come every afternoon until you take the test. Mr. Elam has told me about your desire to be in the fifth grade this semester." Sara pulled out

106

a chair across the table from the lady. *She has an accent, but I can understand her very well.* "Where is your list?"

Sara opened her notebook and showed the lady the list. The lady studied it awhile. Then she smiled at the waiting girl. "My name is Miss Lucinda. I lived most of my life in Mexico. But I attended school in Texas after I was in the third grade. My parents were political people and they traveled a lot. My brother and I went to boarding school in San Antonio. That is why I speak English so well. I spent my summers in Monterrey with my grandparents. That is why I speak Spanish so well." She paused a moment for all this to soak into Sara. "Now, tell me about you and about your family."

Sara began to relax. As she told of their coming to Texas, of living with Uncle Frank and his family, and of now living as a separate family in their own apartment, Sara felt the burden of her despair slip from her slender shoulders. *Yes, I will learn from this one. I can feel it.*

◆ ◆ ◆

Two days later, Miss Lucinda had something in a large brown bag on the table when Sara came for her lesson. Oh, how she wanted to know what was in the bag, but she knew it would be rude to ask. Miss Lucinda acted as though it was not even there. They began the lesson. Sara could say all the words, and now she was having to put the words into sentences. That was hard, for sometimes she would have to learn several new words to make the sentence. Even when she grew tired, she never whined. This was

Friday, and that meant she had only ten more days to fill her notebook with sentences.

"Let us rest a moment, Sara. I can tell you are getting tired. Let us talk in English. You must practice constantly. Tell me about the one-room school you attended on the mountainside. What did you study?"

Sara explained as best she could in English about the parish priest and the missionary lady who took turns teaching the children.

"What subject did you like the most?"

"I liked arithmetic."

"Math, it is called in Texas."

"Yes. I liked Latin, too."

Miss Lucinda leaned over the table as if to hear better. "You studied Latin in elementary school?" In her surprise she slipped into Spanish. Sara was glad. She was tired of speaking in English.

"Our priest loved Latin, so he taught it."

Miss Lucinda shook her head in surprise. "Mr. Elam did not tell me that." She wrote something down on her small note pad.

"He did not know. He did not ask."

Miss Lucinda laughed. "That is not a question one would normally ask an elementary student."

"But I was in the sixth grade. Surely in the sixth grade ..."

"Not in the public schools in Texas. Was it mostly the prayer book and the Bible?" Miss Lucinda's voice still reflected her surprise.

"Mostly, but in the fifth grade we started on Caesar."

"And now you are trying to master your third language. I must tell Amos."

"Amos?"

"My husband. He was the ambassador to Mexico for many years. He retired last year and we moved to the farm of his family."

"You did not wish to retire in Mexico?" Sara knew her family must have been very rich, for political people often were.

"No, we both prefer it here. You and the twins will have to visit me when school is out. They will love riding the ponies." She paused, looked at Sara, then said, "Enough of surprises for today. Now, we must study." But as she took the list from Sara, Sara heard her murmur, "Latin?"

At the end of the session, Miss Lucinda offered the brown bag covered object to Sara. "It is a roast my cook prepared. Sara, when I told her about you, she insisted you had no time to cook a roast. So, she sent this one for you and your family. Please accept it."

Sara was so surprised she could only say "Thank you."

◆ ◆ ◆

It seemed to Sara everyone at Foster Elementary School knew that she was studying for the word test. The students sitting at the fourth- and fifth-grade tables in the cafeteria loved to ask Sara how she was doing. They seemed eager for her to pass. Even the three bilingual students in the fifth grade spoke only English when around her. Sara was so happy. These were her friends. She wondered if Anadelia had done as well in her school. *Has she finally made friends? Do the other students care about Anadelia like the ones at Foster Elementary seem to care about me?*

109

Soon Sara's popularity began to bother Patsy Trumble. Even though Patsy had not done anything to Sara since Anadelia had left, Sara did not feel safe when she was around Patsy. Patsy reminded her of the sleek jaguar that had bided its time before jumping into the path in front of her in the Honduran forest. Yet, as the time drew nearer for taking the test, Sara did not think about anything but the test.

Patsy, it seemed, had been thinking. She had a plan. The day before Sara was to take the test, Patsy walked up to Sara as she was taking her tray to the kitchen window. "You think you're so smart, don't you?"

Sara understood every word, but was so shocked she did not reply, only backed up and stared at the irate sixth-grader.

"Come on, Sara," whispered one of her fourth-grade friends. "Pay no attention to her."

Both girls ignored the fourth-grader. Patsy said, "My mother said the ambassador's wife is training you to be her servant. That she's too cheap to pay regular workers." Patsy's voice rose as she seemed to sense she had cowed Sara.

Sara had moved a step closer to Patsy. "That's a lie. She is teaching me English. And she is a lady." Sara took another step toward the mayor's daughter. "Don't you say ugly things about her."

"My daddy says he's going to tear down those apartments where you and the roaches live ..."

Patsy got no further. Sara knew only that Patsy had put her and roaches in the same sentence. She grabbed a tray from one of the fourth-graders who was listening and tried to hit Patsy with it. Patsy screamed and jumped back, stumbling over a garbage can. She fell to the floor with the contents of the tray all over her. Sara was on top of her and was pulling the screaming girl's hair.

The students who had silently clustered around the two girls began to yell and scream in their excitement. Then suddenly everything became quiet. Two strong hands reached down and pulled Sara off Patsy. "Go to my office at once," Mr. Elam ordered. Sara turned and fled the cafeteria. Mrs. Carrasco flew down the hall after her.

Back at the cafeteria, Mr. Elam was dealing with Patsy. "Quit that screaming, Patsy. You're not hurt," he ordered. He turned to one of the kitchen workers. "Please take her to the kitchen and see if you can get most of that food off her." He shook his finger in Patsy's face. "You get to my office as soon as you're not dripping." He whirled about and headed for his office.

Chapter Fifteen

Sara ran all the way to the principal's office. She could hear footsteps behind her, but she did not look back. She ran past the startled secretary right into Mr. Elam's office. She flung herself into a corner chair. She did not weep. No, it was more like a baby calf bawling for its mother.

She was tired, for she had studied hard the night before. She was frightened by the prospect of failing the test. And now, Patsy had to taunt her, making her lose her temper. *What will Mr. Elam say? What will he do? And Papa! He will be so disappointed in me. And Miss Lucinda. MISS LUCINDA! She'll hear about the fight! She'll think I'm just trash and not deserving of her help.* She began to beat the arm of her chair with her fist. "*Ay mi,*" she moaned as she pulled a tissue from her shoulder bag.

"That's enough of that, young lady," said Mrs. Carrasco. Sara swung around in her chair. The aide stood in the door with her hands on her hips and an angry look on her face. "Go wash your face this instant." She motioned Sara toward Mr. Elam's restroom. Anger, instead of sympathy, from her friend shocked Sara into action. She ran into the bathroom and slammed the door.

"I will wash my face. Then I will go home," she muttered. "I don't have to stay here if I don't like it. I hate Texas. I hate this school. And I hate, hate, hate that Patsy Trumble!" She slowly dried her face and hands. She could hear Mr. Elam talking to Mrs. Carrasco, but she could not distinguish the words. "And I hate English!" She threw the paper towel at the waste basket and missed. For a moment she hesitated, then with a delayed hiccup, she picked it up and placed it in the waste basket.

Sara leaned her head against the door for a moment, not wanting to go out into the office. She knew she would have to face the principal. She could not stay all day in the bathroom. "Be brave, Sarita." Her father's words echoed in her mind. "It is easier with snakes and jaguars," she said. But she pushed open the door and with her head held high, walked past Mr. Elam's desk and sat down.

"Sara, stand up." She stood. She was prepared for the worst. Would he take the paddle to her? The priest used to paddle bad boys when they fought. "Sara, Mrs. Carrasco is going to take you to your house. You and your father will return here at 7:00 tonight. Tell her, Mrs. Carrasco."

Sara's eyes widened in fright when she understood what he had said. "Is he going to do something to my father?" She moved toward the aide as she asked. Fear for herself no longer mattered. Why involve her father?

113

"The principal needs to talk to both you and your father, Sara. He is responsible for your behavior," Mrs. Carrasco replied.

Sara turned to Mr. Elam. "It is the rule?"

"Yes, Sara. It is the rule." Sara felt like she was crumbling inside. She did not resist when Mrs. Carrasco took her arm and led her from the principal's office. All she could think about was that she had shamed her father. Why, oh why, had she not listened to the fourth-grader who had begged her not to listen to Patsy?

Mrs. Carrasco did not speak until they reached the apartment. "I will come by for you and your father at a quarter to 7:00. We will take the twins to stay with Mrs. Beltran. Be ready, Sara."

"You do not have to come for us, Mrs. Carrasco. Uncle Frank can take us."

"I want to be there, Sara. I would not miss this for the world." Sara was shocked to see that Mrs. Carrasco was smiling.

Mrs. Carrasco, seeing Sara's expression, reached over and drew Sara to her in a big hug. "Sara, don't worry. The rule says that the parents of the children who fight have to meet with the principal for a conference. Now, get out. I have to get back to my class."

"Thank you ..." But Mrs. Carrasco did not stay long enough to hear what else Sara intended to say. The car was already down the street.

◆ ◆ ◆

Sara began crying the minute her father walked into the apartment. She had planned how she would tell him. She would be calm and matter of fact. It was something that had happened at school,

114

that was all. But the minute she saw his tired face, her tears began to rain down her cheeks. How could she have done this to him?

Adan put down his lunch box and moved quickly over to where his daughter was standing. "Why, Sarita, what has happened? Is it the twins?" "No," she sobbed. "They are next door playing. Oh, Papa, I have disgraced you!" Harsh sobs tore at her throat. He pulled her into his arms and led her over to the sofa.

"Hush, Sarita. Hush. You will make yourself ill." Sara buried her face in his shoulders. She tried to stop crying. She began to sniffle. He handed her a tissue from the box on the coffee table. "Hush, baby," he pleaded.

Finally, she pulled away from him and straightened her shoulders. "I am in trouble at the school. You have to take me back there at 7:00 for a conference with Mr. Elam."

Sara raised her eyes to his. A questioning look was on his face. "Sara, what happened. What did you do?"

Sara felt the tears rise, but blinked her eyes several times to force them back. "I had a fight." She could not look at him. She began to finger the crease in her jeans. Her hands moved up and down her thighs as though rubbing some of the torment from her body.

"Sara," said her father as he took her restless hands in his. "Look at me." He waited until she faced him. "Now, tell me exactly what happened."

She did. When she came to the part where she was on top of Patsy pulling her hair, she looked away. *What must he be thinking of me?* He placed his hands on either side of her tear-stained face and

115

turned it back toward him. She could not believe what she saw. Her father was smiling!

"A fight? But Sara, you know fighting is not the way to solve a problem. My nose was bloodied many times before I learned that." He pulled her back into his arms and rocked slowly with her. "I'm sorry you are so upset. Why is that?"

"Her father is the mayor! What will he do to you?"

"Yell a lot, probably. But remember, I am a citizen. This is Texas. I may yell a lot, too."

"Papa! Oh, no! What would Mr. Elam say?" Sara pulled out of his arms.

"I will behave, Sarita." He stood and stretched. "Now that I know why my little fighter is so upset, can I go have my bath?"

"Oh, yes. I will put the supper on the table and call Joe and Ester home. Mrs. Carrasco said she would be by at a quarter to 7:00."

◆ ◆ ◆

Mrs. Carrasco was prompt. Sara introduced her father and he thanked Mrs. Carrasco for coming for them. "I would not have missed this for the world," she said in English. Sara knew some of the words, but did not ask her to translate. *Oh, I hope there is no more water in my head. I must not embarrass my father by weeping.*

When they arrived, Mr. and Mrs. Trumble and Patsy were already there. An elderly, white-haired man was standing by the window. Mr. Elam came over and shook hands with Adan. He went behind his desk and sat down. He began his introductions.

"Mr. Beltran, this is Mayor and Mrs. Trumble and their daughter, Patsy. Mayor and Mrs. Trumble and Patsy, this is Mr. Beltran and his daughter, Sara. This gentleman here is Mr. Shelton, one of our school board members. He is one of our local farmers. The rule says at a time like this, one of the board members has to be present. I believe Mayor and Mrs. Trumble have already met Mr. Shelton." The Trumbles nodded and Mr. Shelton came over and shook Adan's hand.

"Now," the principal said, "the business at hand." He turned toward Patsy. "It seems you have a dislike for Hispanics. Why is that, Patsy?"

Sara watched the girl. Would she lie? Would she tell the truth? Patsy looked at her father and mother. Then she spoke. "I feel very sorry for the immigrants. I would like to help them in any way I can." She sat down. Her father beamed at her and patted her shoulder. Sara looked at her father. He placed his hand on her shoulder. His look showed he understood her surprise. Mr. Elam did not look at any of them. He was busy going through some papers on his desk. He pulled several out and then looked at the Trumbles.

"Thank you, Patsy. Now, we will hear from Sara." He smiled at her before asking, "Sara, how do you feel about Anglos? You may speak in Spanish. Mrs. Carrasco, our bilingual aide, will translate."

"Anglos are no different from Hispanics or Asians. Some I like and some I do not." She waited for Mrs. Carrasco to translate. Then she said, "But I should never fight, even when I am very angry. I am sorry."

Mayor Trumble rose to his feet when Mrs. Carrasco translated Sara's apology. "See, she admits

117

it. What are you going to do about it? She could have hurt my child!"

"Please sit down, Mayor. You may speak when I have finished questioning the girls." Mr. Elam did not raise his voice. Sara reached over and took her father's hand. "Sara, thank you for your honesty. Mrs. Carrasco, please explain to Sara that you will tell her later what we are talking about." Mrs. Carrasco did. But Sara intended to listen hard. She might understand some of the English.

Mr. Elam passed out several pieces of paper to Mayor Trumble, to Adan, and to Mr. Shelton. He said, "Mr. Shelton, will you take Mr. Beltran into my secretary's office to make certain he understands these statements from the witnesses of the incident."

To Sara's and her father's surprise, Mr. Shelton spoke fluent Spanish. He led the way to the secretary's office. Mrs. Trumble asked to see the papers. Sara could tell by the frowns on their faces that the Trumbles did not like what they were reading. *What are they reading?*

Several moments passed before Adan and Mr. Shelton returned to the principal's office. When they did, Mr. Elam spoke. "Mr. Trumble, what do you have to say about those statements?"

"Well, now, Mr. Elam," the mayor seemed at a loss for words. "Uh, really, I, uh, need to think about this. Could I have a small conference with my wife and Patsy in the secretary's office?"

"Yes, of course."

Mrs. Carrasco sat by Sara and whispered, "The papers are statements by witnesses of the fight. One of them is mine, too. We shall see how that bigot of a mayor handles this!" Sara heard soft chuckling and

118

looked up to see Mr. Shelton listening. He winked at her and then turned back to the window. *What had the witnesses said?*

From the secretary's office came sounds of angry words. Sara could hear the mayor. He seemed to be shouting something at Patsy. In a few moments, the three of them came back into the room. Patsy looked frightened. Her mother's face was drawn into a scowl. The mayor was plainly embarrassed. His face was red and his nose seemed to be wiggling.

"Well, Mayor Trumble, have you a better understanding of the situation?"

"Well, you have presented a different viewpoint than that I had received earlier of this affair." He took a deep breath and continued, his voice almost a whine. "I checked the rules before we came. I do not believe you have grounds for expelling our daughter." His voice rose as he seemed to gain confidence. "After all, she was the victim."

"She instigated the trouble," said Mr. Elam. "She is equally guilty."

"But you can't expel her," moaned Mrs. Trumble. "It will go on her permanent record."

"Yes, it will go on her record. I did not place on her record the trouble she caused Anadelia Perez. I believed you when you said it would not happen again. But it did." Mr. Elam's voice was very stern. *Now, he is angry, for his ears are turning red. What are they saying?* Sara looked at her father, but he merely squeezed her hand.

"Mr. Elam," began the mayor, but Sara noticed his tone was begging. "Don't you think we're making too much of this little set-to between these children?"

"Yes," added his wife. "Boys fight all the time. Why are we getting excited about a scuffle in the cafeteria?"

"When you called me this afternoon, you insisted I expel Sara. I believe you also said something about checking on Mr. Beltran's employment. I believe you said you would have him fired so he would have to return to Honduras." Mr. Elam was up and leaning over his desk. *He is very angry.* Sara gasped when her father stood up and faced the Trumbles.

"I am a citizen, Mr. Trumble. I am a good worker. I do not think you can have me fired because you are a bigot and so are the members of your family."

Mrs. Carrasco could contain herself no longer. She stood and shook her finger in the Trumbles' faces. "You have gone too far, Mr. Anglo Mayor. We Hispanic Texans are getting ready for the next election, too!"

"Mrs. Carrasco! Please sit down." Mr. Elam said, but Sara saw he was smiling. She could hardly wait to learn what was being said. Everyone was talking so fast.

Mr. Shelton spoke then. "Mr. Elam, I think that Patsy has probably learned a very important lesson. As for Sara, this child has a history of being brave. Now she has learned not to be foolish when she is angry. I see no point in continuing this conference, if both girls agree to control their emotions and beliefs. He paused and looked at the Trumbles for a moment before continuing. "And Mr. Trumble, I think you had better start getting to know your constituents a little better. As a politician you should know there is no room for prejudices of any kind."

"Ah, yes, I understand. Perhaps my daughter misinterpreted my views somewhat." He was beet red as he spoke. Mrs. Trumble sat with eyes downcast, her fingers opening and shutting the clasp on her leather purse.

Patsy turned an angry face toward her father. "But I heard you say ..."

"That's enough out of you!" Mr. Trumble stood and yanked on Patsy's arm. "It's time we went home." He looked at Mr. Elam's impassive face. "Come, Grace, as far as I'm concerned, this meeting is over." He nodded in the general direction of the others and pulled his family from the room.

"What is happening, Papa?" Sara could stand the suspense no longer. "Tell me, please."

When Mrs. Carrasco and Adan began speaking at the same time, Mr. Shelton called for quiet. He was grinning and so was Mr. Elam. Sara knew they certainly were not angry with her. Mr. Shelton drew up a chair near Sara and began to explain in Spanish.

"Sara, I think your actions either helped the mayor become a better politician or ended his career. Either way, it was for the best. He had infected his daughter with his bigoted views for too long. But," he wagged his finger at her, "you, too, must not be so sensitive. There will always be those who, because they choose to be ignorant or mean, will speak ugly things about immigrants or people who are different."

Mr. Shelton went on to tell her what had taken place in the room. "Mr. Beltran," he addressed her father who had sat quietly all the while, "my wife has nothing but praise for your daughter."

"I do not understand." Adan turned to Sara. "I did not know you knew Mrs. Shelton."

121

"I don't, Papa." Sara was equally puzzled.

"I forgot," said Mr. Shelton. "You only know her as Miss Lucinda. She was in the cafeteria shortly after the fight. She was determined to be here, but I convinced her it would be better for me to come." He chuckled. "She can get very emotional at times. I did not want her attacking Mayor Trumble. Now, let us include Mr. Elam in our conversation." He waved his hand toward Mr. Elam as though returning control to the principal.

"Everything explained?" Mr. Elam asked as he stood and stretched. "Thank you for coming, Mr. Shelton. Having a board member present was a very good idea. Now the mayor can't say we took advantage of his daughter." He walked around the desk to where Adan and Sara stood. "And thank you, Mr. Beltran, for your patience. I hope this meeting has convinced you that we at Foster Elementary try to be fair in handling our problems."

Adan smiled. "I know my children are in good hands here at this school." He turned to Mr. Shelton and offered his hand. "Thank you for being here. I am anxious to thank your wife for all the help she has given Sara." He placed his arm about Sara and pulled her to his side. "She is a good daughter. We have been through some bad times together. She has always done more than her share."

"Then," said Mrs. Carrasco, with a sigh, "let us go home now so that Sara can get a good night's sleep. She will have to be very alert for the test tomorrow."

"The test!" Sara said in English. She had forgotten about it. "*Ay mi!*" she moaned. The men laughed at her expression.

Mr. Elam walked them to the door and patted

Sara on the shoulder. "I don't think you have anything to worry about, Sara." Adan softly translated what the principal had said.

"Thank you, Mr. Elam." Sara followed her father out to the front of the school.

Mr. Shelton said, "Lucinda wanted me to get permission from you, Mr. Beltran, to have Sara and the twins over to the ranch Saturday."

At that moment, the thought of being out at their ranch brought no joy to Sara. Her mind was on the test she would have to take the next morning.

Chapter Sixteen

When Mrs. Carrasco stopped her car in front of Uncle Frank's house, all the Beltrans came running out to meet Sara and Adan. In spite of the cold weather, no one had stopped to put on a coat or sweater. "Come inside, please. All of you," insisted Aunt Rosita. "I have refreshments."

Everyone crowded around the kitchen table. The twins were hanging onto Sara. Both were begging to know what would happen to her. Finally, Uncle Frank ordered, "BE QUIET! Let Adan tell us what happened."

"In Spanish, please," Alma begged as she smiled at Sara. "The English will be too hard for Sara." Sara smiled gratefully at her cousin.

Adan explained, first to the twins, "Nothing is going to happen to your sister. Except," he smiled as he looked at Sara, "perhaps she will not be so quick to fight next time."

"Never, Papa," Sara whispered as she leaned against his shoulder. Then he and Mrs. Carrasco took turns describing the session in the principal's office. "You should have heard Mrs. Carrasco warn Mayor Trumble." He repeated what the irate aide had said. Everyone laughed.

"It is time someone of us spoke up to that bigot," Uncle Frank said. "And you, Rosita, don't laugh. You have not registered to vote."

"But I do not want to serve on the jury," she complained as she looked around the group for support.

"They also choose jurors from the property tax rolls, too." Mrs. Carrasco looked at Aunt Rosita as she spoke. "You are the owners of this house?" Aunt Rosita glumly nodded.

"Even so, Rosita," Uncle Frank said as his fist hit the table. "You are a citizen. You have that responsibility. You must do your duty." Sara could tell that Uncle Frank appreciated being a citizen of the United States. He had accepted his responsibilities.

"Oh, yes, Mrs. Beltran. You must register." Mrs. Carrasco looked at Adan. "And you?" she asked.

"I will. After meeting the present mayor, I certainly will register to vote."

Finally, it was time for Sara and the twins to go to bed. To Sara's surprise, Alma took Sara's hand just as she was leaving. "I will pray you pass the test, Sara."

"Thank you," was all Sara could say. She could hardly wait to tell her father that Alma was going to pray for her!

♦ ♦ ♦

125

When they arrived at their apartment, Adan put the twins to bed. "You, too, Sara. It's time for you to go to bed."

"But I have to study some more."

"Sarita," he said, "you need your sleep more than you need to study. You will do all right on the test tomorrow." Sara fell asleep immediately after Adan sent her to bed.

The next morning Sara was rested and calm. "I did what grandmother said to do," she told her father at the breakfast table. "I asked the good Lord to help me. I will do my best. The rest is up to Him."

"You did well to trust Him to help you. I, too, prayed for what is best for you." Adan hugged her, then picked up his lunch box and left for work.

◆ ◆ ◆

Mrs. Welch smiled when Sara entered the first period ESL class. "You are ready?"

"Yes." Sara did not feel nervous. It was as though she were merely facing a daily quiz. Mrs. Welch took Sara into the teachers' workroom. "You will not be disturbed here." She handed Sara the test and the extra notebook paper Sara would need for writing sentences using the selected words. "Do you have two pencils?"

"Yes." She had not been allowed to bring her knapsack into the workroom.

"Take as long as you need," Mrs. Welch said.

Two hours later, a tired but excited Sara handed back the test and the papers with the sentences to Mrs. Welch.

"Through so soon?"

"Yes. I thought I would have to write 600 sentences. But I had to write only fifty. *Ay mi!*" She gave an exaggerated sigh of pleasure.

"You deserve to pass, Sara. I know you have really studied hard."

"When will I know?"

"Monday morning."

"Not until then? How can I wait that long without knowing?"

Mrs. Welch smiled in sympathy. "The weekend will pass quickly, Sara. So, enjoy it. If you pass to the fifth grade, you will have to really study to keep up with the other students. Enjoy your weekend. Do not worry."

Sara walked swiftly toward her third-period class. *I have to wait until Monday!* Then she remembered she and the twins had been invited to spend the day with Miss Lucinda and her husband at their ranch. *Surely*, she decided, *that will make the weekend pass a little faster.*

The weekend did go by very fast. Not only did Mr. Shelton provide Shetland ponies for the twins, but he also had a gentle horse for Sara to ride. And they went swimming in the lake nearby, too. Sunday, Adan insisted they all go to the Spanish language service at the big church downtown.

Chapter Seventeen

Monday morning, Sara could hardly eat her breakfast. "Papa, what do you think?"

"I think you have nothing to worry about. But, whatever happens, Sarita, it is the will of God."

"Yes, Papa."

Mrs. Welch met Sara at the door of the ESL class. Before Sara could ask about the test results, Mrs. Welch said, "Mr. Elam wants to see you in his office right away. Now, give me your knapsack and hurry."

Sara turned and hurried toward the principal's office. The faster she walked the faster her heart beat. *Why does Mr. Elam want to see me? Has Mayor Trumble changed his mind and wants the principal to expel me? Is Patsy still complaining?* She did not think about the test results. To her, being sent to Mr. Elam's office meant TROUBLE!

There was no one in the secretary's office. The

door to Mr. Elam's office was closed. *Should I knock?* Sara hesitated for a moment, then straightened her shoulders. "Be brave," she told herself, echoing her father's words. She tapped softly on the door and then stepped back. *Maybe he is busy. Will he be angry that I am disturbing him?*

Just then the door swung open. "Why, Sara, you are early. Come on in." She followed him into the office and sat in the chair held for her. "Now, let me see. Oh, my," he said. "Where is Mrs. Carrasco?" Before Sara could translate what he was saying, there was a knock on his door.

"Come in," he called, for he seemed to know who had knocked. Mrs. Carrasco came into the office. Her broad smile helped to still Sara's fears. Without waiting to be told, Mrs. Carrasco pulled up a chair beside Sara.

"Well," she asked, not waiting on the principal to speak. "Did she or did she not?"

"Just a minute, please. Her test is here in this stack of papers." He ducked his head and shuffled through the many papers on his desk. Sara thought her mind would explode with impatience. She was glad she was only there about the test. *But why does he not hurry?* "There, now. Here it is."

She thought she might die before he finally said, "Sara, I'm proud of you. You certainly passed this test. Mrs. Welch and I were both amazed with the sentences you produced." He handed her the test to study. "Mrs. Carrasco will go over it with you while I attend to a problem back in the cafeteria." He left the office. Sara looked at Mrs. Carrasco, who was reading the sentences she had written.

"What did Mr. Elam say?" Sara had understood the "passed the test" part, but not the rest of the words.

Mrs. Carrasco told her what he had said. Then she placed the test papers back on the desk. A surprised but pleased look was on her face. "I cannot believe you did so well in such a short time."

Sara was so happy she could hardly speak. "Miss Lucinda told me I seemed to have a gift for languages, or else learning Latin really helped me with the English." Sara was so happy she could hardly speak. She leaned back into the chair and sighed. "I wish my mother knew."

"What makes you think she does not?" Mrs. Carrasco handed the test papers to Sara. "Look those over. When you finish, I will make a copy for you to take home and show your father."

Just before Sara finished reviewing the test and the scoring, the secretary came into the principal's office. "Hello, Sara. Congratulations. Here is your new schedule. You will still report to Mrs. Welch's ESL class, but you will come at the second period." She looked to Mrs. Carrasco to explain the new schedule.

"I will go over it with her, Bonnie," said Mrs. Carrasco. "Will you make a copy of these papers for Sara?"

"Certainly," the secretary said.

When Sara got home that afternoon, she wanted to do something special to celebrate her promotion. To her surprise, there was a note in the grocery money jar under the cabinet. Her father had placed it there the night before. Written in Spanish, it read: "Dear Sara. Do not go to the grocery store. Do not cook supper. We have a surprise for you." It was signed, "Papa."

Why did he write the note? A surprise for me? Was he that sure I was going to pass? Or did he think he would have to cheer me up if I failed? Sara sat at the kitchen table and wondered and wondered until Joe and Ester began to pester her to play with them.

Two hours later Adan came home from work. "Well?" he asked when he put his lunch box on the table where Sara was sitting.

She tried to say it calmly, but her joy in telling made her shout, "I did it! I passed the test! Tomorrow I will be in the fifth grade!" She ran to his side and began hugging him. She begged for him to explain the note.

"Your Aunt Rosita and your Uncle Frank have invited us all over for a celebration supper."

When Sara and her family arrived, she was overjoyed to discover Alma and Roberto were both home. Alma gave Sara a pair of earrings. Roberto gave her one of his flashy T-shirts like one that Alma wore. Sara was thrilled by both the gifts. Uncle Frank and Aunt Rosita gave her another Sunday dress from the resale shop. Tears of gratitude filled her eyes as she looked at her father. "I love you all," she whispered.

"I, too, have a gift, Sarita. Tomorrow, the telephone men will install a telephone in our apartment. And I promise," he grimaced at his brother, "not to fuss when you sit for hours talking to your new friends."

Before they sat down to the celebration supper, there was a loud honking from the driveway. No one moved toward the door to see who was honking in the driveway. Everyone kept talking as though they had not heard. When there was a loud knock on the door, no one went to answer the knock. Sara looked around the living room. Everyone was smiling. Aunt Rosita said, with a sly grin on her face, "Sara, please

131

answer the door," Sara obediently moved to the door. Just as she got there, it opened.

"Lupe! Ronaldo! Papa! The baby is here!" Sara was almost jumping with joy as the visitors made their way into the living room. No one was sitting. Everyone was up hugging someone. Sara's sparkling brown eyes silently pleaded with Lupe, who understood. She handed Sara little Francis Adan Maria Beltran.

Sara looked at Aunt Rosita as she gently hugged the baby. "This is the most wonderful time in my whole life. Thank you."

"Your victory celebration would not be complete without a reunion with those who came with you to Texas," Uncle Frank said.

♦ ♦ ♦

The next morning, Sara went to Room 134. Mrs. Daniels, her new homeroom teacher, met her at the door. "Come in, Sara. We have been expecting you."

Once again Sara turned and stared into twenty-two pairs of eyes. She remembered the fear she had felt that first day in the fourth grade. *Changes. New rules to learn*, she thought. *Had it been a good idea to leave the fourth grade?* She was frightened by the thought of having to start over again. New teachers. New students. Harder subjects. Then she remembered her father's advice. "Be brave, Sarita." She now knew that being brave around wild animals was almost as difficult as being brave in the world of people. Yet, as she stepped through the door to the fifth grade, she knew it was worth being brave to be an English-speaking citizen of the United States. She was very proud to be called a Texan.